GAY MEN'S PRESS

Air From Other Planets

Andrew Clements

Air From Other Planets by Andrew Clements

First published 2000 by Millivres Ltd, part of the
Millivres Prowler Group, 3 Broadbent Close, London N6 5GG

World Copyright © 2000 Andrew Clements

Andrew Clements has asserted his right to be identified as the author of this
work in accordance with the Copyright, Designs and Patents Act 1988.

A CIP catalogue record for this book is available from the British Library.

• **ISBN 1 902852 13 3**

Distributed in Europe by Central Books,
99 Wallis Road, London E9 5LN

Distributed in North America by InBook/LPC Group,
1436 West Randolph, Chicago, IL 60607

Distributed in Australia by Bulldog Books,
PO Box 300, Beaconsfield, NSW 2014

Printed and bound in the EU by WS Bookwell, Finland 2000

'We have lingered in the chambers of the sea'
T S Eliot

'I feel air from other planets'
Stefan George
Enrapture

One

The huge hibiscus flower stood out amongst the other airline logos like Carmen Miranda at a cabinet meeting. Pink and purple, forty feet high and dripping with tropical pleasure, it was a veritable beacon shining from the aircraft's tail. The moment Mark saw it his spirits lifted, a frisson of anticipatory delight shot through him and he was drawn irresistibly like a moth to a nightlight.

He turned into the departure lounge and through it's great glass wall was granted a view of the entire plane. 'My God' he thought 'a DC8 ... it's a fucking DC8! Who ever would have thought it? Well, how wonderful, how absolutely wonderful.' He hadn't realised there were any still flying and eagerly approached the glass for a closer inspection. He always felt a bit soured by the efforts airports made to anaesthetise the experience of air travel or to foil any sense of excitement the traveller may have, but it had to be said that most did not let you down when it came to this point. He had said his goodbyes to Phyllis and left her at the barrier only minutes before, but she was already gone from his mind, at least for the moment, as he stood poised now on the brink of communion, practically nose to nose with the object of his passion and once again deeply impressed by the scale and sheer physical presence of the thing.

Mark loved aeroplanes. All his life he had loved aeroplanes. Even as a young child it had been far more than a mere boyish interest; it was an obsession, mystical in substance, and it had dominated his life. The fact that he wasn't capable of flight himself had been the greatest frustration of his early years. After all, birds could do it. Whole afternoons were spent hurling himself off chairs, convinced that if he tried hard enough he could manage to dangle above the ground, even if just for a few precious moments. But no, his best efforts always ended in failure and a five year old's consummate rage.

But up in his bedroom there was always the other world, the one where he spent most of his time, the one where anything was possible and he was in full control. It must have been a million times that he launched himself stylishly out of his bedroom window, swooped down over the patio, levelled out across the rose beds and looped the plum tree before soaring out over the lawn in a glorious arc to a nicely controlled landing at his hideout in the big apple tree, which was really a secret helicopter pad. His father had built this platform in the convenient natural crow's nest of the tree and it quickly became a great sanctuary. From here he could plan and execute reconnaissance flights over neighbouring gardens. If a longer range aircraft was available he could go further afield, perhaps even to Hemel Hempstead, though of course that meant taking a navigator along.

By six-and-a-half he was tall enough to climb over the coal bunker and up onto the flat roof of the garage. This not only allowed him to survey the entire garden from on high, but also offered an uninterrupted, all round view of the skies and it was here that his two worlds magnificently collided. Mark grew up very near to not one but two aircraft factories whose various products would buzz his house on a daily basis. The familiar roar of jet engines, just a couple of miles away, always meant something was going up and it was his signal to go springing out on to the garage roof where he would sit, transfixed as a Victor bomber circled the village, never more than a thousand or so feet up. Sometimes he was the controller, enthroned in the tower with the aerodrome spread before him, directing the take-offs and landings. Sometimes he was the pilot, easing the controls and guiding the plane over the fields of Hertfordshire. Usually though he just sat and stared, mesmerised by the fantastic machine and the magical fact of it's suspension above the ground.

As for actually going up there, that was to remain a fantasy until his mid-teens. Thanks to an enterprising teacher at his school a chance came for a group of boys to go up in a glider. However, this produced a tidal wave of emotions that overwhelmed his delicate fourteen year old sensibilities and his aerial baptism, on a cool October evening, saw him floating above the Dunstable Downs for twenty minutes in a state that bordered on apoplexy. Soon after this a foreign holiday with his parents meant a flight from Luton to Barcelona. But a seven hour delay amidst crowds of irritable and unexcited people, followed by the event itself taking place entirely at night, combined cruelly to extract most, if not quite all of the anticipated cosmic pleasure. In the real world of air travel so many things conspired against him: fear, motion sickness, boredom, claustrophobia, and - worst of all - other people. So Mark continued to enjoy his flying in a world where these things didn't trouble him, a world where he could skulk freely around aerodromes, take off, sail over the countryside, land, take off again, and all the time be in absolute, singular, blissful control.

*

"You'll hate it you know."

"Shut up Phyl." Mark regarded his aunt with a measure of disdain.

"Bill hated it."

"Bill was working. Anyway, the man's got no soul, we both know that."

"It'll be bloody hot and bloody humid and you'll bloody hate it. You just see if I'm right." Twenty-three years of living in Sydney had expunged all traces of the wholesome, home counties voice he remembered from childhood visits. She spoke now with an acerbic, nasal twang that grated in his ears like a fork on china. There she sat, across the table from him, straight backed, smoking passionately and looking nothing like her sixty-two years. After college Mark had come out to Australia in a grand effort to see more of the world. In between periods of hitching around he had lived on and off with his aunt and uncle and during this time he and Phyllis had become soul mates. She would punch him on the jaw if he ever tried to tell her what she meant to him, but she was alone amongst his relatives in being utterly unfazeable; he could talk to her about anything at all, no matter how down to earth or personal it was. Once he was safely back in England she became the first and almost the only person he ever told about his sexuality. The long, drunken letter had taken all his courage to write but the reply had come within a week, on a postcard! 'Dear M - for God's sake if you're going to write a letter at least give me some bloody news. Love P.'

The nervously hoped-for relief had been enormous and had actually brought tears to his eyes. But it had also been short-lived. If Phyllis had known all along that he was gay, if it had been so obvious to her then it must surely be obvious to others too. He wasn't prepared for this, the panic hit him like a sledge-hammer and rapidly evolved into a deep self-consciousness that had stayed with him ever since. In moments of despair he would write to her and she always answered promptly with the same lecture about how he didn't ask enough of life and how he couldn't go on for ever being frightened of everyone. But the courage she inspired never lasted more than a day or two. The awful self-consciousness she had unwittingly planted in him was now deeply rooted and coiled around him like ivy, quickly smothering any flicker of resolve.

The Captain Cook Lounge was one of Sydney airport's saving graces. A huge window gave directly onto the apron, offering a splendid view of the aircraft in their earthly manoeuvrings. Today it was pleasantly unbusy and they were able to sit right by the window and look out at the planes. He ordered a cold lager, she a white wine. But Phyllis being

Phyllis she had a wine box stashed in a holdall under the table and would discreetly refill her glass whenever the barman wasn't looking.   "It's going to be wonderful" said Mark, with as much cool assertion as he could muster.

"Yeah ... right."

"Anyway" he said "life should be an adventure don't you think?"

"Oh, well, that's good coming from you."

"What's that supposed to mean?" He knew exactly what it meant, but tried to put as much effrontery into his voice as he could get away with. She ignored him.   "Still, I don't suppose we would have seen you if it wasn't for this little obsession of yours."

"Not true."   Mark spoke with indignation. "I'd really missed Sydney. Getting back here was number one on the list when the money came through. I mean come on Phyl, I hadn't seen you for seven years, talk about withdrawal!" She gave him a withering look. He blew her a kiss.

"Pity about the old girl though" she said.

"Oh come off it, you hated her."

"Other way round, more like. She always thought Bill had married the village tart."

"And did he?"

"Well of course he did, but that wasn't the point. She thought he'd married beneath himself, that was the point. That was why the miserable bitch never spoke to me."

"Still, history eh? She left me three grand you know." Phyllis kept an eye on the barman while she bent and refilled her glass.

"She left all of you three grand."

"Well at least we all got the same. Just imagine if all us grand-children had ended up with different amounts, that would have set things cooking."

"Cooking? Darling, this family's already cooked. Boiled over, burnt and stuck to the bloody pan if you ask me."

They both laughed and drained their glasses. Mark stood

up. "I'll get another round in before that barman gets too suspicious."

"Anyway" he said, placing the fresh drinks on the table. "What was that remark about me not being adventurous? You talk crap sometimes don't you."

"It's not crap young man, it's the plain truth. Life's passing you by and well you know it. For God's sake when are you going to get yourself a boyfriend?"

He attempted an expression of mock chagrin, but it cut no ice, so he let his gaze wander out over the airfield. "Yeah ... well ... it's not that simple."

Sure it's simple, get out more."

"Out? What do you mean 'out'? I'm sitting here on the other side of the world for Christ's sake, how much more 'out' do you want?"

"You know what I mean." She fixed him with one of her looks.

"Yeah, OK. But it's still not easy."

"Well my dear, you're not the first person on Earth to find that out. Promise me you'll start making more of an effort, I only want to see you happy, that's all."

"I am happy."

She regarded him coolly. "Bollocks" she declared.

*

He stood close to the glass and considered the DC8 before him. It was an aged machine, of that he was in no doubt; signs of decay and battle-weariness were evident all around it's body. But inspite of this tired appearance it still seemed full of power and the potential to thrill; and faced as he was with the ridiculous cheerfulness of it's vibrant and seductive colour scheme any anxiety he may have had about it's airworthiness just evaporated away.

Mark had stood here many times before, in many different

airports around the world. He had relatives scattered all over the place and over the years had made good use of them. Offers of free accommodation, whether unsolicited or carefully engineered, had considerably stretched his travel budget so that now, at the age of thirty three, he was a seasoned frequenter of long-haul routes. He had seen wonderful things from aircraft: sunset over the Rocky Mountains or the jungles of Sumatra, icebergs in the Arctic Ocean, dawn coming up over the Himalayas or the red centre of Australia. And for all the misery of queuing in crowded airports or the long hours of boredom, especially on night flights, that little flame of childhood wonderment had never quite been extinguished. It flickered now as he stood, tantalisingly close to this amazing machine.

He had flown out of Sydney at least half a dozen times before, but either on short domestic flights or to face the gruelling twenty-four hours back home to London. Today was very different. Today was fantastic. Today was the climax after a year of dreaming, a year of obsessing and wondering about a place as enthralling and mysterious to him as any childhood lost world fantasy.

He surveyed his fellow passengers. Young, most of them; fun-seekers off to the surfing beaches and night-clubs of Honolulu. But why did they all look so bloody miserable? Did they not realise what was about to happen to them? Did they not fully understand that they were going to climb into that large metal tube outside and be rocketed out over the ocean and away up into the stratosphere? Surely no-one could be so lacking in imagination as to be unmoved by such a prospect? Poor souls. He wasn't sure whether to be cross with them or to feel pity, so he turned his back to them and resumed his solitary communion.

It was November and the afternoon was bright and hot. From the air-conditioned world behind the glass the heat beyond was tangible. The air shimmered thickly over the aircraft's fuselage, above it's wings, above the tarmac beyond. A 747 stood poised some distance away, monstrously massive and seemingly alive. The captain opened his throttles, the four engines drew breath and it hurtled down the runway with a crackling roar that shook the building, steam pouring from it's wings. When at last it tilted and lifted, improbably, above the ground Mark lifted with it and followed as it soared away. Soon it was nothing more than a speck, high in the sky, but his eyes remained glued long after it had disappeared completely into the ether. A stirring behind him quickly became a surge of movement that brought him suddenly back to earth. Two hundred people were rising and gathering their various belongings. The gate had opened and Mark's pulse had quickened.

Two
A year earlier

It was pouring with rain. Mark had got soaked through just running the short distance to his car. In the morning it had been quite sunny and he hadn't thought to bring an umbrella, but the high pressure had been elbowed aside during the day by a deepish low and Maddingly New Town lay shivering now under a dreary blanket of grey cloud that relieved itself unconcernedly over the dim streets.

It was half past three and already trying to get dark. He had managed to get away early from work and was looking forward to an afternoon at home - a pot of tea and a leisurely read of the paper while he luxuriated in a nice hot bath. There was much to lament about Maddingly New Town but traffic jams were not generally one of it's problems. But today there was clearly some obstruction down on the motorway and everything was at a standstill. He hadn't moved for twenty minutes - not an inch. It could only be an accident, he thought, nothing else could cause this kind of mess. Some stupid arsehole going too fast in the rain. He didn't mind them killing themselves but look how many people they inconvenienced. 'Stupid bastards' he said aloud, several times.

Big trucks loomed on either side of him, massive, growling and hissing their frustrations. Rain drummed on the roof and the heater whirred away valiantly, failing to keep pace with the condensation that lay an insistent claim to his windows. Every few minutes he was obliged to take a cloth to the windscreen in order to gain a view of the large van in front. It's grimy back doors announced a landscape gardening firm from Gloucestershire and he wondered idly what they were doing all the way over here in Essex.

But Gary Dromer dominated his thoughts. Gary Dromer always dominated his thoughts as he drove home. Over the last six months it had become a ritual for him, always the same, like a daily mantra mentally chanted as he made his familiar way along. When he arrived home it was always the same - everyday - he would peel away his office clothes and relieve himself in leisurely contentment while in his mind Gary Dromer took merciless possession of him.

Mark had never forgotten the moment six months before when he had turned from the coffee machine towards his usual chair by the window in the refectory to find this stranger sitting there. Startlingly handsome with an open, vibrant face, his black hair closely cropped and his body muscular and rangy. When Mark sat in that chair he made little impression on the rather firm cushion, the muscles in his legs giving slightly at the sides and he had been immediately struck by the way this man's thighs remained perfectly integral while digging purposefully into the cushion. That night he had slept little, unable to stop laving those powerful thighs with his tongue or reverently munching an assumedly huge and rubbery mound of genital flesh through thin cotton briefs while the stunning stranger nonchalantly considered what to do with him.

The next morning he had been sitting at his desk, staring at his screen, struggling with his piece on the fire. Some youths had set a shop on fire a couple of nights before and a guard dog had unfortunately been caught in the flames. Mark disliked dogs with a passion and longed to imbue his column with subtle hints of quiet satisfaction, but the community at large had been horrified and his attempt at a sensitive piece had run to eight hundred words. Philmore had sent it back with a typically curt note - he only wanted four hundred and reminded Mark for the umpteenth time that this was the Maddingly Chronicle and not the "fucking Observer".

But when the door opened and the beautiful newcomer

walked in the plight of the roasted rottweiller evaporated from his mind. Buzzingly athletic, the man approached Mark with a large hand purposefully extended. "Yeah hi, Gary Dromer, new ads man, good to meet you." They shook hands and Mark marvelled at the controlled power in his grip.

"Hi" he replied, standing, blushing. "Mark Fletcher, new-shound." He laughed self-consciously and felt completely ridiculous. 'Why do I let these things come out of my mouth?' he thought - 'Why oh why oh why?' In the next five minutes he learned that Gary had been newly appointed to manage the small ads section, that he worshipped West Ham United, played football himself on Sunday mornings as a matter of religious observance with training on Wednesday nights while 'the missus' looked after their three children at home. That he was as oblivious of his own attractiveness as he was of weather conditions on Venus and that he was very possibly the most completely heterosexual man on Earth. After he left Mark had tried to re-focus on the shop fire but it was hopeless; he spent the rest of the morning spread-eagled naked on a bed while Gary Dromer looked down at him, his strong face grinning smirkily, a can of lager in one hand and Mark's testicles in the other.

At lunchtime he had gone out for a walk and this had helped to clear his head. In the afternoon he had managed to get a bit of work done, but as he drove home his mind teemed with thoughts of the stunning Mr. Dromer and his erection strained painfully in his lap. For the first time in a long time he was in no doubt about what he would do when he got home.

And so it began - the daily commuting round filled with desperate longings and endless, unrequited obsession. Today, sitting quietly in the rain and relieved of the need to focus at least part of his attention on the road ahead, Mark was able to concentrate more fully on his image of the wonderful Gary Dromer and to savour the anticipation of what he would do when he got home. His hand rested idly in his groin and there he felt the warm flesh stirring and filling. He was chilled and fed up in this miserable weather and his swelling sex was something of a comfort.

Lost for a moment, and almost without realising what he was doing, he unbuckled his trousers and unzipped his fly. His fingers went in and began to explore, to appreciate the flesh, urgent beneath the cotton of his underwear. But they weren't his fingers that dug in and teased and stretched, they were Gary's and he was sprawled on a bed, struggling to keep still as he'd been instructed. Then a wicked idea came to him. He realised that no-one could actually see him - no-one at all - he was penned in by high-sided trucks and his windows were comprehensively steamed up. 'Go on' he whispered to himself - 'no-one can see you.' With that he lifted the waistband of his shorts and his willy gratefully emerged, free and clear. He didn't look down at first, but he felt the air around it, cool and thrilling and he began to knead and stroke the flesh with his fingertips.

A sudden shifting of the blurred and foggy shape beyond the windscreen shocked him abruptly back to himself. The traffic was moving - the reality of it intruded sharply and he felt a quick pang almost of revulsion. 'Look at yourself' he said out loud - 'just look at yourself, a grown man wanking in a traffic jam, for Christ's sake put it away!' He felt painfully silly and quickly did himself up, looking anxiously around, though no-one could possibly have seen what he was doing. He hated being flustered and made an effort at least to appear nonchalant for his non-existent audience as he tried to regain his composure. Sensing the insistence of the car behind he wiped the windscreen, slipped into first gear and eased slowly forward.

It was gone five when he finally turned into the driveway and made a dash through the rain to the front door. He had lost a good hour in the traffic, but as he shook out his raincoat and hung it up his only thoughts were of a cup of tea, a long soak in a nice hot bath and the enjoyment of his delayed communion with an imaginary Gary Dromer. 'Thank God for central heating' he said out loud as he made his way upstairs - 'thank God for central heating.' He stood in the bedroom and began to undress while Gary sat on a stool across the room watching, grinning hugely. When Mark was down to his underpants he hesitated, toying with the elastic waistband. 'Not these as well' he pleaded.

'Everything' ordered Gary, 'come on do as you are told, I want to have a good old look.'

Mark leaned forward and stepped out of his underwear, his flesh responding immediately to the first shock of nakedness under Gary's imagined scrutiny. Standing up straight he put one hand behind his back and with the other slowly pulled his skin back so as to offer maximum vulnerability. For a few moments he stood still, legs apart, hands behind his back, submitting to Gary's inspection and wondering what exquisite tortures he would be subjected to tonight. But just then the telephone rang. Worse than that - he knew it was her. He always knew when it was her. A bizarre telepathic link existed between them through the telephone line. He knew it was her and she knew he was at home. And she knew he knew she knew. But how was it, he wondered, that she always managed to ring just as he was masturbating? It was uncanny - as though she had some kind of sixth sense about it. No matter what the time of day, she regularly managed to catch him just at the worst possible moment. He always started out resolutely determined not to answer, but she was amazing, she wouldn't hang up even if he let it ring for ten minutes and then she would speak with the same innocent, sing-song voice that was always so maddening, yet at the same time so immediately disarming.

Gary had evaporated with the first ring. By the third Mark's willy had withered like a deflated toy balloon and he reached for his towelling robe, hurriedly covering himself up.

It was a horrible feeling - as though his mother were there in the house. There was nothing to be done - he lifted the receiver.

"Oh hello dear, only me."

"Oh hello mother, how are you?"

"Yes, yes, mustn't grumble. How are you dear?"

"Oh you know - muddling through." It was a tape loop and they had been playing it for fifteen years, the same lines exactly time after time.

"Listen dear it's Nanna - she's had another turn, they think it's bad this time. She's back in Queen Elizabeth's." That 'Nanna' always grated. She couldn't say 'your grandmother' or 'granny Fletcher' or 'Winnie'. Her own mother had always been 'granny Smith' and she still thought this was hilarious after thirty-odd years, but her mother-in-law she persisted in calling 'Nanna'. He knew she did it for the same reason she still called him 'the boy' in front of other people. In his teens he had railed against her but her serene implacability had caused him even more stress so he had long since given up protesting and now tried simply to rise above it. This was easier said than done however and he still flinched every single time.

And he knew very well what was coming next:

"I wondered, I mean if you aren't doing anything in the morning, you couldn't run me could you? I would be awfully grateful dear, I mean I don't often ask and I really think she hasn't got long."

'Bugger' he thought - that was his Saturday gone. Immediately he felt guilty. It wasn't that he didn't care about his grand-mother, of course he did, but he couldn't help his knee-jerk reaction. The trouble, to Mark's mind, was that they all acted as though this was some unexpected tragedy. Winifred Fletcher was ninety-three, she had led a very full life, understood the situation perfectly well and was thoroughly positive about it. In the years since Mark's father died she had never really enjoyed good health. Now her heart was weak and she was very tired. Mark honestly believed she was quite looking forward to going. And it wasn't at all that he didn't want to see her, it was just that he would rather have had time with her when his mother was not present.

"Oh no, poor old girl" he said. "Yes okay mother, I'll be round about elevenish."

He pulled up outside his mother's house at quarter past eleven and beeped his horn. At the very same instant she erupted out of the front door and, slamming it behind her, came marching towards him with rigid shoulders and the coldest of expressions.

"Really Mark I do think you might try harder" she said, climbing into the car.

"Mother what ever are you talking about?"

"It's quarter past and we did say eleven, I mean we did say eleven."

"I said elevenish, you didn't say anything." He loved to torment her like this. He lived with the fond conviction that if he kept it up long enough, if he really was systematic and relentless, that cracks would eventually appear; that she might at last begin to understand how pointless this all was, and perhaps even to relax a bit. He knew she had got out of bed at eight precisely and that her whole morning had been a countdown to his arrival at eleven, moreover that this schedule had been meticulously planned the night before. He knew that she had been ready at ten thirty and had begun waiting, growing twitchier as the clock ticked. He also knew that she knew he would be late - anything from five minutes to half an hour. 'Actually mother I was late on purpose because I knew it would irritate you.' He had often toyed with the idea of saying something like that to her, but he understood very well the effect it would have - any glimmer of reality intruding into their relationship would instantly cause her to short-circuit and she would not absorb the information anymore than if he spoke to her in Hungarian.

"One of these days dear, one of these days."

"One of these days what?" he replied with a mock sneer - he knew perfectly well what was coming next.

"One of these days you're going to find a good woman, that's what, yes and she'll keep you in order, you just mark my words. Anyway she's getting worse Mark. Leonard rang me this morning. He's had a call from the hospital, they think it could be any time now. Everyone's going up there."

Mark felt really guilty now, but his mother's last phrase bothered him more - 'everyone's going up there' - the words echoed in his head. He hated family gatherings at the best of times. Something like a lunch party was bearable, as long as it didn't happen too often, as he could hide in a corner and get drunk while they all wittered on vacuously, pretending they actually liked each other and the world was full of white people. But an occasion like this where reality had to be dealt with was altogether more difficult. Mark knew how uncomfortable it would be, how obstructive the awkwardness, not allowing him to say goodbye to his grandmother in the way he would like. And he was sure too that it would be the same for all of them. A procession would be much better - solo audiences, five minutes each. But that would be out of the question, they would crowd round the bed in a great pretence of family unity, none of them able to say what they really wanted or needed to in front of the others.

"I tried to phone Bill this morning but there was no answer."

"Mother you can't afford to phone Australia, I'll phone Bill and Phyl. Anyway, Leonard's probably rung them already."

"You don't have to ring them dear, it's quite all right. I can afford it."

"Mother..."

"No, no, I insist Mark." She only called him by his name when she really wanted to drive a point home.

"Mother it's okay, really. I haven't had a decent gossip with Phyllis for ages." He realised straight away that he was twisting the knife but the words had just slipped out.

"MARK!!!" she barked at him, much more loudly than she had intended. "That's all you can think about at a time like this, bitching with that bloody woman!" She opened her handbag and burrowed in amongst it's contents. They both understood that the conversation would stop there. Admittedly he had goaded her, but she had overstepped the mark, broken the unwritten rules of their engagement and they would speak no more until they arrived at the hospital. She shrivelled slightly in her seat and twitched occasionally.

They heard Leonard long before they turned the corner and saw him. Red-faced, he towered over an extremely tense-looking ward sister who stood, hands clasped in front of her, looking straight into his eyes as he offered her his view of the situation.

"Three people? Three people!!? Listen girlie I'm a taxpayer, I pay your wages, we (indicating the room) pay your wages. That's my mother in there, my mother!! dying!! and you don't fucking tell me who she can and who she can't have round her bed, do you understand? Do you understand?" She looked down, then quickly up again.

"Mr Fletcher I..."

"GOOD!!" He slammed back into the room and the ward sister, composing herself with difficulty, strutted away.

Winifred Fletcher lay motionless on her back like a beached walrus, blue-faced, her enormous stomach rising and falling slightly as she breathed. Plastic tubes were everywhere - in her arms, in her nose - several emerged from under the covers at the side of the bed and Mark preferred not to speculate on the parts of her they might be attached to. Behind her a bank of machines beeped and winked. She was deeply asleep.

Apart from Winifred there were five people in the room, not as bad as Mark had imagined. They all sat huddled round the bed - Leonard and Rosemary, Leonard's sister Marjorie, her son Tony and Tony's wife Clare. They all looked round, nodding, smiling glumly as Mark and his mother came in. Only Leonard spoke...

"Angela ... Mark ... there's a machine down the hall if you want a cup of tea." They both smiled at him but neither answered. Tony stood and offered his chair to Mark's mother but she motioned that this wasn't necessary and instead took up what she fondly imagined was a supervisory position at the foot of the bed. Mark skulked at the side of the room, leaning uncomfortably against a shelf piled high with boxes of thin rubber tubing.

His mother and uncle Leonard both stared concernedly at Winifred. Rosemary and Marjorie exchanged troubled looks across the dome of the old lady's belly, Clare studied the floor intently and Tony gazed vacantly at the twinkling machines. Nobody spoke. Winifred's breathing was the focus of all their attention. Slow, shallow and a little erratic, it was accompanied by a quiet and rather unsavoury rasping noise. After about fifteen minutes or so, by which time Mark was beginning to feel more than a little mesmerised, Winifred breathed in as normal but then failed to exhale. Panic flashed round the room. The five rose as one from their seats and a tight ring of heads closed over the bed as though pulled by a drawstring. For a few ghastly seconds nobody breathed; but the old lady's lungs creaked again, the drawstring was cut and the five fell back into their chairs with perfect synchronisation and a rush of sighs. A few minutes later it happened again - the creaking stopped, the ring of heads closed, breath was held then released copiously as Winifred clung on to her life. Then it happened again ... then again. The fifth time was too much for Mark and an enormous chuckle erupted out of him. He managed to convert it instantly and, he thought, rather brilliantly into a fake cough and hurried out of the room. A nurse going busily by with a bed pan stared wide-eyed as he burst through the doors, clutching his sides. Guilt stung him terribly, but it only made the whole thing tickle all the more. He sat on a chair and tried to compose himself but the giggles were as untamable as bubbles in boiling water, he shook helplessly and struggled to regain his composure. After some minutes, looking up through water-filled eyes he saw his mother staring down at him with a look of terrible disappointment.

"She's gone Mark ... Nanna's gone."

Three

Standing to the side of what was called, rather too grandly he thought, the Main Operations Room, Mark's office was a quiet little enclave that, albeit glass-walled, was never-the-less all his own. When he first arrived at the paper he had been offered a desk in the bustle of the main room but quickly spotted this little retreat. Nobody seemed to know why it was unoccupied and since it boasted not only a desk but a functional computer as well he wasted no time in claiming it as his own.

So he sat, in happy isolation, tightening up his article about Reverend Anderson. The local vicar, much loved by his congregation although well-known to be mildly eccentric, had been stealing lead from the roof of his own church and selling it to a local scrap dealer in order to raise funds towards the very same church's restoration. It seemed he had been at it for several months before an eagle-eyed constable finally spotted him late one night prowling between the flying buttresses. Mark was having great fun playing with possible headlines, none of which would ever have got past Philmore: 'Local vicar is two hymns short of a prayer book.' 'Local vicar is two wafers short of a communion.' 'Local vicar is lead astray.' 'That one might get in' he thought, 'even old pig-eyes can't be that boring.'

Just then the door opened and the bald head and small piggy eyes of Nigel Philmore peered round. "Ah Mark - got your note. Very sorry and all that."

"Thanks Nigel..." Mark couldn't disguise his surprise. "Still, it wasn't such a shock really, I mean she was terribly old and she'd been ill for ages." The editor nodded slowly in an effort to appear concerned.

"Still, no fun eh?" Mark was dubious whether Philmore

had any concept of fun. "So the funeral's Thursday, yes I don't see any problem with that, and it is the whole day you want off is it?" Mark gave him a look that he hoped said 'yes of course I want the whole day off for my own grandmother's funeral if that's not asking too much you fucking miserable bastard.'

"Yes, yes, well I'm sure that'll be fine Mark. Fine. Oh yes, I brought your Venice piece . I expect you know what I'm going to say."

"Yes Nigel I know what you're going to say" Mark sighed - "'This isn't the fucking Observer'"

"Well it isn't Mark. For goodness sake, how many of these things have you given me - fifteen?"

"Eight."

"Eight, well, aren't you ever going to realise it's just not the sort of thing that would work in the Chronicle? Every time you go on holiday you come back and write one of these ... these pieces, and every time I tell you the same thing. If you want to get this sort of stuff published send it up to the woofters in London."

"But..."

"Look, Mark, I have nothing against the piece, it's a very good piece, it's just that it's ten times too long."

"But I've said to you before Nigel, why not have some sort of supplement or an occasional series of longer articles on subjects of general interest? Whatever could be wrong with that?"

"But this sort of stuff is just not what our readers want Mark, no-one would read it."

"Well who's to say what they want? You read it."

"That's different."

"Why is it different?"

"Mark ... all our readers would want to know about Venice is how much it costs to get there, how much it costs to stay there, what the best package deals are, when is the best time of year to go and how to order spaghetti bolognese. You've got them drifting quietly into St Mark's basin while buildings emerge ghost-like through a gently rolling sea-fog."

"What I actually wrote was..."

"And four whole pages about a fruit market!"

"A floating fruit market."

"What's the difference?"

"The Rio San Barnaba is a uniquely fascinating place."

Oh I'm sure it is, but Mark - three of those pages are about a pile of aubergines."

"Well you just don't see aubergines like that anywhere else, they're amazing - purple and sensuous and..."

"And what is all this moralizing about tourists?"

"What about it?" After fumbling for the right page Philmore held it out as though it were someone else's handkerchief. He read aloud...

"'The traveller is an adaptable creature, motivated by boundless curiosity, happy to follow wherever it leads and to suffer for it if necessary. The tourist's curiosity on the other hand, while genuine enough, is constrained by clear boundaries which relate to comfort and effortlessness'" He paused and looked down at Mark who met his gaze and said "Yeah ... and...?" Philmore continued, his tone balanced somewhere between mockery and vitriol. "'If tourism and travel have anything in common it might be their inherent sadness, but these are very different sadnesses. Chance plays it's part in the progress of the traveller who, in his transient state is apt to have contacts with others that may be intense but are inexorably short-lived. Tourists and their hosts on the other hand remain effectively detached from one another, each acting out roles in a pre-planned scenario. The traveller proceeds with an open heart and mind, stimulated by the potential limitlessness of opportunity and ready to be changed by experiences. The tourist is the antithesis of this and suffers from brochure-induced myopia...' and so on and so on, there's pages of it!"

"Well I thought that was all rather good" said Mark, although he hadn't been concentrating fully. Gary Dromer had just walked slowly past the window and the greater part of Mark's attention was focussed on the ladder of creases that moved in the fabric of his chinos between the two round mounds of his bum. Philmore dropped the manuscript on to Mark's desk , his lips curled inwards and his eyebrows raised in an expression that suggested there was nothing more to say on the matter. He backed away and opened the door.

"No more of them eh Mark. Send them to the woofters in London if you like but don't give me this stuff anymore." With that he departed, irritatingly leaving the door ajar.

Almost in the same instant Gary's face appeared in the doorway. "What's the matter with him then? Miserable old sod. Didn't get his balls in last night, that's what, not like you and me eh Fletch?" He winked and grinned and disappeared. Mark was dumbfounded. 'So Gary doesn't think I'm gay?' He reeled as the reality of that thought struck him. Mark believed the whole world tacitly assumed he was gay and because he couldn't bring himself to be open with anyone he constantly worried about what they secretly thought of him. But Gary evidently saw him as someone who 'got his balls in' every night. What a revolting expression, he thought, images passing through his mind of sweaty scrotums being squeezed like toothpaste tubes and emptying their contents into some woman's clammy crevices. He grimaced and shivered at the thought. But Gary probably believed everyone was heterosexual - unless you actually wore a dress or something - and just because he 'got his balls in' every night he naturally assumed everyone else did the same.

'So he thinks I get my balls in every night' Mark mused. 'So who does he think I get my balls in with? Does he think about me having sex?' He noticed a slight quickening of his pulse...' no of course not, don't be stupid, he just assumes that I do.' But Gary's words continued to ring in his head and a much more astringent realisation dawned on him. Of course it had been unconscious on Gary's part, Mark was certain of that, but nevertheless he had clearly made the implication that the two of them had had sex together - '"not like you and me eh?"' Mark heard the words over and over again, so close to being a tangible link between real life and his endless fantasy world. His eyes returned to the VDU. 'Local vicar is lead astray.' Yes, he would definitely go with that, he thought, and if Philmore didn't like it he could jolly well stick it up his clammy crevice.

Mark did have sex once - sort of. Whenever he looked back now on the event he could never quite take in that it had actually happened and he still wasn't exactly sure how it had. It was four years ago and he had not been at the paper long when he was asked to go to a small house in The Granaries, a new estate on the outskirts of town, to interview a young couple who were trying to get a neighbourhood watch scheme going after their garden had been vandalised. Actually it was the police who were getting the scheme off the ground but the couple had appealed to the Chronicle to help publicise their cause and Mark was duly dispatched to obtain their story.

The photographer who came with him was a young man called Freddie Stapleton. He had not been working at the paper long either but they had been out on several jobs together and Mark had found himself powerfully attracted. Freddie had a neat, healthy looking body; a lively, open face with a cheeky grin and he always wore well-cut jeans that showed off his strong legs and lovely little bum to great advantage. Around the office he was something of a jack-the-lad, giving the cheerful impression that he didn't give a shit about anyone and this quickly made him universally popular. But when Mark began to spend time with him driving to and from various assignments he started to see a gentler side to the young man.

He fantasized freely and frequently about Freddie. In his imagination the two of them had acquired an extremely thorough knowledge of each other's anatomy, had scaled great heights of passion and driven each other to exhaustion through long sessions of sexual frenzy. But Mark soon began to suspect that Freddie might actually be gay. It wasn't any-thing specific - nothing he could really put his finger on - it was just a feeling. It occurred to him that it might just be the result of him wishing and imagining very hard, but as soon as the idea was there he stopped fantasizing so much, nervous even at the smallest hint of reality, or of real potential. Several times he felt that Freddie had held eye contact with him for just frac-tionally longer than was necessary or appropriate, and maybe that he had even noticed a twinkle in those boyish eyes. But the idea that Freddie Stapleton was not only gay but actually interested in him was so patently ridiculous that he tried very hard to make it go away.

They spent about half an hour with the young couple, Mark listening to their tale of woe and Freddie taking pictures of them standing glumly over their ravaged flower beds. Driving back, Mark mentioned casually, and without really thinking about it, that he only lived a few streets from where they were. "Does that mean you're offering me a cup of tea then?" Freddie asked, cockily. Mark felt a little knot of panic form inside him, tiny but unmistakeable. He made an effort to look nonchalantly at his watch and heard himself say "sure, why not?" A minute later they were pulling into his driveway.

Mark's house wasn't really untidy, it just had a lived-in, not-quite-on-top-of-the- housework sort of look. He liked it like that, he thought it was homely and comfortable. He never could stand to go into pristine show-homes where he was uncomfortable putting a mug down for fear of spreading infec-tion in the surgical cleanliness. His mother's house was like that. But whenever anyone visited him he always felt slightly on edge, as though he needed to apologise for the state of the place. He had tried to tell himself that this was stupid, that his home was just that - his home - and if someone didn't like it they could jolly well bugger off. But he never quite managed to shake the feeling, especially with strangers or people who hadn't been there before, that his private space was somehow being violated, exposed, scrutinised. Also it was strange to be at home during the day when he would normally be at work, it always reminded him of being ill as a child and having to stay home from school - a faintly surreal sense of the atmosphere in one's familiar surroundings being oddly changed.

He stood in the kitchen rinsing out some mugs. "Tea or coffee?" he shouted, but turning round he saw Freddie in the doorway staring at him. A moment later the photographer was at his side. "Come on Mark" he said quietly, "when are we going to stop mucking about..." he hooked a finger under Mark's belt and pulled him closer "... and start mucking about?" The little knot that had been in Mark's stomach since they were in the car erupted and shot through him, numbing his mind and rooting him to the spot. What happened next was a blur - all he could remember later was hot smoky breath, a tongue probing his mouth, fingers everywhere. Somehow they found themselves up in his bedroom, tumbling on the bed in a flurry of flying clothes. Mark had dreamed a thousand times of another man's hand reaching into his underpants, but when Freddie's fingers snaked in and curled around his willy the poor thing shrank away to a little cashew nut and the more he worried about the other's disappointment the more it shrank and shrivelled. He was stifled by a screaming self-consciousness. He worried terribly what Freddie would think of his body or of his performance. He was paralysed by a white and blinding panic. Freddie kept telling him to relax but it was hopeless - he wanted to apologise for everything but couldn't get any words out. Even his normal ticklishness was gone. All he was aware of was the weight of the other's body on top of him, a tongue that wasn't his swirling in his mouth and a great deal of urgent fumbling. After a while the young photographer groaned, his body stiffened and his semen lay warm and sticky on Mark's stomach. He found it repulsive and was grateful that Freddie quickly got some tissues and mopped it up.

"I don't know why you look so worried" said Freddie, "that

was fun." Mark felt the hollowness of his words like a blow to the temple. He desperately needed to be on his own. He was pleased that Freddie got dressed quickly and immensely relieved when he said "I've got some bits and pieces to do down town so I'll hop on the bus - don't worry about a lift back. See ya later." With that he left the room , slipped down the stairs and was gone from the house.

The instant he heard the front door close his panic disappeared as though it had never been there. He stretched himself on the bed and imagined Freddie's fingers playing over him, tickling, tormenting. Freddie's scent was everywhere, it filled the room and was powerfully erotic - half way between a fantasy and a physical presence. He breathed it in, gripped his erection and tossed himself joyously. Afterwards he put a tracksuit on and came downstairs. It was already three-o-clock and he couldn't contemplate going back to work after what he had just been through. He rang in and told them he had dropped Freddie off and come home with a migraine. He made a cup of tea and sat down on a stool.

He was shell-shocked by what had happened. The photographer's hurry to get away had certainly been humiliating but underneath Mark had a definite sense of relief. The afternoon's events, while absolutely unexpected, had confirmed what he had long known - if half sub-consciously - that he was not really capable of enjoying a sexual relationship with another. It was all too difficult, too complicated, too much to think about. When he fantasized and masturbated he was always in control, always focussed on his own body with no distractions. He didn't have to think about doing things to someone else, to worry about whether they were having a good time or doing what they really wanted. He could do what he really wanted, in his own time, at his own pace and his fantasy companion would behave exactly as he required him to. He had always half suspected that this was the case, now it had been proved to him and he believed beyond any doubt that for better or worse he would always be alone.

He finished the piece about Reverend Anderson, snappy title and all, saved it and switched off his screen. He looked at his manuscript lying forlornly on the desk where Philmore had dropped it. All right, he thought, the stuff about tourism was a bit wide of the mark but the piece as a whole was brilliant. He had been to Venice several times and each time had wanted to write about it but had always been overawed by the subject, never knowing where to begin or quite what it was he wanted to say about the place. A fiction might have worked, it was always at the back of his mind. It would have allowed him to be more poetic, to let an abstract and powerful sense of the place seep through the narrative and make the reader ache to be there. But he had never been able to think of a story.

This time though the writing just seemed to flow out of him. He had only gone to Venice for a quick three day break, but on his last evening there a remarkable thing had happened. He had sat in a quiet bar on a corner of the Campo San Bartolomeo and got slowly but thoroughly drunk with cheap red wine. It was one in the morning when he stumbled out into the maze of alleyways and canals and before long he was completely lost. Not that he minded in the least. He lurched around the dark and quiet city for a very long time until at last, and quite suddenly, he found himself in St.Mark's Square. He stopped dead in his tracks and marvelled at the splendidness of it as though he were seeing it for the first time. It was a few moments before he came fully to himself and understood what was strange. The full realization was amazing - there was nobody there - not a single soul, save for him. He was standing in one of the most revered and gorgeous architectural sites in the whole world, immortalised by Canaletto, visited by millions of tourists each year, and he was quite alone. He walked slowly to the centre of the Square, facing the Basilica, and sat down cross-legged on the cold flag-stone floor. He breathed deeply of the damp, musty air; listened in disbelief to the silence and, not at all convinced that he wasn't dreaming, attempted to absorb the reality of this unexpected and monumental privilege.

The following day he flew home, an uneventful flight over thick cloud that denied him a view of the Alps. The best part for Mark had been to notice the way the 757's long fuselage flexed during take-off as though it were a living, fleshy thing, stretching and relaxing into it's stride. He arrived home in the early evening and sat up most of the night writing. He was sure that this would be the one - this would be the piece that would change Philmore's mind, would melt his heart and make him see what such writing could do for the Maddingly Chronicle. But alas, Philmore's ignorance had surpassed all expectations. He brought his manuscript home and consigned it to the drawer with all the others.

Four

Driving home one evening he decided, on the spur of the moment, to call into the library. He hadn't read anything much for a while and fancied picking up a novel or two to help while away the evening. Trawling along the shelves he came across a very thick volume with 'RLS' on the spine in large letters. He took it out, for no particular reason and found it to be a compendium of four novels by Robert Louis Stevenson, complete with a potted biography. Treasure Island he had read at school. The Strange Case of Dr Jekyll and Mr Hyde he had always known was written by Stevenson, though he had never read it and hadn't even known it was called that. But there were also two shorter novels included in the collection, neither of which he had heard of - The Beach at Falesa and The Ebb-Tide. This all looked rather fun to Mark and he decided there and then to take the satisfyingly plump volume home with him.

He knew nothing at all about Stevenson, except that he was Scottish and although the biography that served as an introduction to the book was potted to say the least, he was immediately compelled by the image that emerged of a very good-looking and brilliant man who, suffering terribly with tuberculosis, had left Scotland and travelled to the other end of the earth in search of a climate in which he could breathe. He learned how Stevenson spent time in America, having married an American woman and then, in response to an editor's commission, undertook a great ocean voyage around the South Seas in a trading schooner. That subsequently he had made two more such voyages before finally settling in Samoa, only there finding a climate sufficiently benign to offer a measure of relief from the misery of his oppressive illness.

Without knowing very much more than that and without having read any of the books Mark found himself drawn in by Stevenson. Perhaps because he was half way through a bottle of Chianti by this stage and his creative juices were flowing rather freely he could sense, in his fascination with the man, the makings of a new project - a very long term project - to read every word Stevenson wrote, research the man's life meticulously and write the definitive critical biography. That was if someone else hadn't done it already, and he had no idea whether they had or not. He took a piece of cheese from the fridge, poured himself another glass and settled down to lose himself in The Ebb-Tide.

Immediately he was gripped by the Boys-Own story of three vagrants and ne'er-do-wells washed up in a South Sea island backwater, stealing a ship in a moment of desperation and sailing off in search of a way out. Desperate men marooned in an alien world, forced into desperate acts in order to keep afloat. In the expanse of the South Pacific a hundred years ago they could still have had some hope of disappearing and starting a new life and Stevenson's evocation of glittering islands and great ocean spaces was a revelation.

The writing was wonderful - every sentence beautifully balanced, every phrase exquisite. It was just like Conrad only more readable. But this story of people driven to extreme behaviour in order to survive in an alien world was, he felt sure, the basis of everything Conrad had written, and Graham Greene and plenty of others. And Stevenson pre-dated them all. He was completely enthralled and devoured the pages voraciously.

'The sky shaded down at sea-level to the white of opals; the sea itself, insolently, inkily blue, drew all about them the uncompromising wheel of the horizon. Search it as they pleased, not even the practised eye of Captain Davis could descry the smallest interruption. A few filmy clouds were slowly melting overhead; and about the schooner, as around the only point of interest, a tropic bird,

white as a snow-flake, hung, and circled, and displayed, as it turned, the long vermilion feather of it's tail. Save the sea and the heaven, that was all.'

He stopped at this passage and read it over and over again. He was more than enthralled, he was there, floating along with Davis and Herrick and Uncle Ned in that great watery emptiness. He heard the creaking of the old wooden ship and smelt the warm, salty air. He felt the void stretching around them, he stood with these men and felt their freedom, their fear, their desperation.

One of the crew fancied he had sighted land and '...*pointed to a part of the horizon where a greenish, filmy iridescence could be discerned floating like smoke upon the pale heavens.'* This wasn't taken at all seriously by the others, yet was too tantalising for them to ignore. The man had seen something similar before and was most insistent. Amidst much scratching of heads a South Seas navigation guide was consulted and although on the chart they appeared to be in the middle of a great empty space it offered speculation about a pearling island in roughly that position '*which from private interests would remain unknown'* and whose existence was not accepted by South Sea sailors and traders. The possibility was there that they had happened upon a secret island, a tiny coral atoll, because light from its lagoon was reflected momentarily in a passing wisp of cloud. Although just a few hours sail away they would never have seen it otherwise. They were far from convinced, but it was all too enticing for them so they brought the ship about and pointed her bows towards '*...that elusive glimmer in the sky, which began already to pale in lustre and diminish in size, as the stain of breath vanishes from a window pane.'*

Mark had finished the whole bottle of wine by this point and realised that if he read any more he would simply nod off. So he cleaned his teeth, swallowed a large glass of water, climbed into bed and drifted off to sleep, his head swimming with ocean swells, wooden ships, warm air and fabulous, jewel-like islands.

At work the next day he found it hard to concentrate, but for once this was not because of Gary Dromer; instead his mind kept floating away into the dream-world of the South Pacific. He sailed for weeks across an expanse of blue ocean, he sprawled on powdery white beaches, he heard the coconut palms rustle in the tradewinds and watched a tropic bird swoop vermilion against a blue, blue sky. At lunchtime he sat in the park with his sandwiches and read on. There really was an island there and when it proved to be inhabited by a man - Attwater - infinitely more canny, sophisticated and calculating than any of the three Mark could guess that their enterprise was doomed. But it wasn't that that blunted, albeit very slightly, his urgency in reading the book, it was his realisation that this was, in essence, a re-working of an older, true-life story. Desperate men deeply out of place, stealing a ship in a moment of mad impulse and casting out to sea, finding a secret, uncharted island and hoping to find sanctuary there - this surely was the story of Fletcher Christian and the Bounty. The famous mutiny was one of those odd things, one of those peculiar flashes of history that had long fascinated him, had long sat at the back of his mind as something that would be really interesting to explore one day. Stevenson had given him a sudden fascination for the South Pacific and that had been the key that opened the flood-gate. The desire to investigate this particular episode of naval history now rushed in like tidewater and saturated his already swirling mind.

The following day, mercifully, was Saturday. He got up early, caught the train to London and by lunchtime was back at home with maps of Tahiti, Samoa and Tonga and three thickish books, all devoted to the story of the Bounty mutiny. By Sunday night he was an expert. He had devoured all three volumes and knew just about all there was to know about that ill-fated voyage.

But he had many questions that the various writers either failed to address or at least didn't offer any theories about. Captain Bligh was evidently a brilliant seaman and had a reputation for being one of the best navigators in the navy. But he was not, as was usual with officers, from the aristocracy or educated classes. All the commentators had him as a blunt, rough-hewn character who had worked his way up through the ranks by virtue of his natural ability at seamanship. Many of his crew on the other hand, and just as unusually for ordinary seamen of the time, were educated men who had volunteered for the trip. But why? Mark wondered. None of the writers gave any consideration to this or could help him at all. Presumably they had simply wanted the adventure, but he couldn't help feeling that there was somehow more to it. He had already half forgotten about Stevenson and the seeds of another project were germinating in his mind.

The voyage out had been very hard. The *Bounty* sailed from Portsmouth on November 28th 1787 but only got as far as the Isle of Wight where they were forced to anchor in a cove, sheltering from atrocious weather for nearly a month before finally managing to get out into the Channel on the day before Christmas Eve. But again the ship was battered by terrible seas and they were obliged to put into Tenerife for repairs and refitting. During the long run down to Cape Horn Bligh restricted the already meagre rations because he was uncertain how long the voyage to Tahiti might take. The men might have accepted this reasoning, but the rationing was so tight that they suspected him of a simple meanness of spirit. Several incidents occurred on board in which the ferocity and irrationality of Bligh's temper further dismayed and alienated the men. At Cape Horn they battled horrendous weather conditions for a full month before turning and running with the prevailing winds through the Southern Ocean. They arrived near the Cape of Good Hope on May 23rd and spent a month at anchor, repairing the ship from the ravages of the voyage. A cold, hard passage of two months followed before they sighted the Mewstone Rock and made landfall in what is now Tasmania. There they were forced to fell trees and saw them into planks in order to further repair the ship. They finally reached Tahiti on October 25th 1788 after a voyage of ten months and twenty-seven thousand miles, a miserable and deeply disaffected crew, half starved and having suffered great humiliation at Bligh's hands. At one stage even one of the officers had been flogged, which was unheard of in naval history.

Mark could only wonder at the courage and resilience of these men. They were the astronauts of their day, he thought, the Star Trekkers, casting off into the ocean wastes, maybe to find uncharted lands and unencountered peoples. Braver perhaps than today's astronauts as they had no contact with home, or possibly with humanity at all for many months; no communication, entirely dependent on their own resources and on each other.

Tahiti must have seemed beyond paradise to these men. The warmth and lushness, the intense physical beauty, the abundance of food, the friendliness and uninhibited sensuality of the people. The Bounty was here for five-and-a-half months while it's cargo of breadfruit plants, bound for Jamaica as cheap food for slaves, grew large enough to be transportable and the men slipped quickly and easily into the Polynesian way of life. Bligh did nothing to discourage this and indeed appeared to have completely misjudged the situation, failing to understand the depth of his crew's attachment to the place or the extent to which many of them had become enmeshed in Tahitian life. Leaving it behind, returning to sea and to the grim realities of close-quartered ship-board life must have been agonizing for them, the more so under the privations of Bligh's draconian regime. His approach to the situation was to apply discipline even more harshly. As the men grew more and more unhappy he attempted to exert evermore ruthless control. If only he had known about catastrophe theory, thought Mark. If a more

sophisticated man had been in charge the mutiny would probably never have happened. Fletcher Christian's famous cry
rang in Mark's head:
*"I am in hell! I am in hell! I have been in hell for weeks past and I
mean to stand it no longer!"* But maybe Mark was being unfair
on Bligh, maybe he didn't know enough about it all yet.
Stevenson's biography was receding into the distance as a new,
radical view of the mutiny on the Bounty presented itself as a
possible challenge for his research and literary skills.

The *Bounty* sailed from Tahiti on April 4th 1789 and the
mutiny took place after only three-and-a-half weeks at sea,
early in the morning of Tuesday 28th, about thirty miles south
west of the island of Tofua in Tonga. After setting Bligh and
those loyal to him, or at least to King George, adrift in the
ship's launch, Fletcher Christian and the other mutineers
returned to Tahiti. There he set down those men who had
taken no part in the mutiny but for whom there had been no
room in the heavily overloaded launch. Several of the mutineers also chose to remain in Tahiti while Christian took his
band of renegades and disappeared into the wide Pacific.

It was two years later that the long arm of the admiralty
again reached Tahiti as *HMS Pandora* came looking for the
mutineers. Bligh's open launch was so overloaded it had sat a
mere six inches out of the water, and yet, navigating from
memory as he had no charts, he had succeeded in sailing three
thousand six hundred miles to the Dutch East Indies from
where he and his crew were able to find a passage on a ship
going back to Europe. A remarkable feat which still stands
today as a record distance for an open boat voyage. But some
of the mutineers who remained in Tahiti had, during this time,
also done a remarkable thing. They had felled some trees and,
having only the most primitive tools available, constructed an
entire thirty-five foot schooner. This ship, named *Resolution*,
proved not only to be thoroughly seaworthy, but was faster and
more manoeuvrable than the *Pandora* and robust enough to

make light work of long ocean passages. In the years to come this little yacht was employed in the pearling trade around South-East Asia and at one point made the fastest ever sail passage from Taiwan to Honolulu.

But how, Mark wondered, was it possible for a handful of men to construct such a craft entirely from scratch using only a few primitive axes, no proper tools, nothing to measure with, no glue, no metal fixings, just supreme carpentry skills. These men had wit and intelligence and were evidently craftsmen of exceptional, almost breath-taking ability. So what were they doing working as ordinary seamen on the Bounty? Mark was convinced there must be a great deal more to this story than was ever previously understood. But even as he toyed with the idea of researching it another, even more exciting idea was forming in his mind. A fiction. Yes. All sorts of strands were coalescing for him around the story of the *Pandora*, which was almost as remarkable as that of the *Bounty* itself. He had no idea whether this would turn out to be a novel, a short story, or whatever, but over the next few days the routine of work became a singular intrusion as his mind raced and teemed with ideas. He didn't make notes, that wasn't his way. He just allowed the ideas to form and play about and settle down in his head.

By the time Friday evening came he was ready to begin. He was deeply excited, though in a serene sort of way. He warmed up some left-over curry in the microwave and ate it standing in the kitchen. Then he made a large pot of tea, found a packet of chocolate biscuits, retrieved two thick file pads from his briefcase, along with a clutch of ball point pens he had pinched from work, sat down at the table, spent some minutes composing himself, and thus he began:

'William Wilkins made his way along the track. He had been walking for some hours and in all that time had not met another, not a single soul. The heat of the afternoon was great and the air he found exceedingly moist, more so even than in Apia, where he had

stayed since his arrival one month before. In his twenty five years of life he had scarce travelled at all, annual visits to his aunt in Bristol having afforded his only opportunity for an excursion outside London. The long carriage journey, two days with good horses, had always felt like a great adventure. His application to the Missionary Society had been made largely at his father's urging and for his own part with great scepticism that he would receive a posting at all. His surprise when summoned to the Society's offices in Paternoster Row was considerable and his reaction upon learning of his commission is better imagined than described.

A passage had been secured for him aboard a frigate of His Majety's Navy which was to sail from Portsmouth one month hence on a charting voyage to the South Seas. He would leave the ship at Apia, in the Navigator Islands, there to join the missionary James Smith and support him in his work.

It was the summer of 1834 and it was spent in a whirl of preparations and desperate farewells, but the long sea voyage, five months in all, proved to be a time of tranquillity and reflection for him. He would spend hours in his cabin reading his Bible. He walked the decks and gazed for long periods at the ocean. The activities and rhythms of shipboard life went on around him but did not much affect him. He dined with the captain and officers, there enjoying many pleasant evenings of conversation.

Upon arrival in the Navigator Islands he found himself plunged into a world wholly and utterly alien to him in every respect. The heat was tremendous and his English clothes ill suited to it. The air he found smotheringly damp but the light was of a clarity and brilliance such as he had never encountered in England. Every plant was strange to him, not one was familiar. Many possessed leaves of such monstrous proportions that their physical presence fairly intimidated him. But his greatest experience of shock was afforded by the natives themselves. Tall, well-made and handsome, unselfconsciously naked, or very nearly so, and to a man possessed of the most affecting serenity. His desire to go amongst primitive peoples and bring them to the Lord had been driven in part by a fond intention to raise them, through spiritual awakening, out of the misery of their situation. Instead he found a co-operative and peaceful society with an abundance of resources, a placid lifestyle and a general serenity and contentment that he fancied most English people would greatly envy.

James Smith was a quiet, rather aloof man who had not known of William's assignment and was not especially pleased to receive him. He was the only white man in the islands and had been there in all for five years. The native people seemed to respect, even to revere him and he had, at least locally in Apia, achieved not inconsiderable success in spreading the word of God. When William confessed to him that he felt more than a little embarrassed by the apparent contentment of the people and wondered quite how he was going to help them, James reminded him sharply that while they may appear outwardly content, their souls still required to be saved and that a knowledge of the Lord would only enhance and enrich their admittedly pleasant lives.

James told William that the islands had first been sighted by white men in 1722 when a Dutch ship passed nearby. The navigator - a man called Roggeveen - charted their position incorrectly and so the name given to the islands seemed somewhat ironic. He thought it more proper to refer to them by their collective native title - Samoa. The island they were presently on, William learned, was called Upolu and the larger one a few miles to the west was known as Savai'i. It was there that James required William to go, to live among the people, learn their tongue and their ways and eventually to bring them to the Lord. Doubtless also to get him out from under his feet.

Thus a large canoe was organised and a group of young men enlisted to row him across to Savai'i. They set off early one morning and the crossing took all day. Arriving at a suitable beach an hour before sunset the young men set to building a fire and supplemented the fresh water and fruit they had brought along with a skilful display of spear fishing. The party all slept in the body of the canoe and in the morning they directed William to a track through the rainforest which they said would bring him to a village in two hours of walking where he would find nice people who would treat him well.

As he continued along the path he began to hope the fellows had not mislead him about the distance to the village - or indeed that he had not misunderstood them. His knowledge of the native tongue extended to only a few words thus far, but he was certain his journey should involve but two to three hours of walking. He had presently been walking for more than four and was keenly in need of a rest and of refreshment. He carried some fresh water in a gourd in his bag but it was almost all used up. He also carried a large knife and had been taught how to open a coconut but he had found none lying near the track and was certain he could not climb a tree for one as he had observed native boys doing.

He was starting to become more than a little fearful of his situation when, through an opening in the trees to his right he looked down to see a pretty curving beach and, not far from shore, a man fishing from a small canoe. The sea in that place was perfectly calm, being protected by a reef of coral and as he watched, the man threw a net over the water, waited a minute or two, then hauled it in and picked over it's contents before once again spinning it out over the water.

William's spirits rose at this sight for he knew that he must indeed be close to the promised village and that relief was therefore at hand. He left the track and picked his way down the hill through the undergrowth to the little beach where he sat, watching the fisherman and thinking that the fellow must break at some time and come ashore and that he would then introduce himself.

But something intrigued him. He had not, in the weeks he had been in Samoa, seen a single native who did not have hair of the blackest hue. Yet this fisherman's hair was pale - almost white in fact - and even at a distance he could clearly see that the hair was straight and not thickly curled as all natives' hair was. The man was as dark-skinned as any Samoan, but he could not as yet make out any features.

At length the fisherman was satisfied with his trawl and started for the shore. On catching sight of the missionary, now standing,
waiting for him on the beach he stopped rowing abruptly and stared
in a most determined manner. Indeed he appeared to William rather
as a startled rabbit in the moment before he bolts for cover. William
could see now that the man was elderly, though still of a robust
frame, but he was yet too far off for his features to be clearly made
out. For his part the man had recovered from his shock and was
making for the shore with alacrity. As he beached his canoe and
climbed out onto the sand William was astonished to see that he
was indeed not a native at all. Although he wore nothing but a simple cloth wrapped around his waist in the native fashion and his
skin was of a gloriously dark hue, it was obvious from his face that
he was of European stock. The fellow strode up the beach, laughing excitedly and as he approached with his hand outstretched in
greeting William was even more astonished to find himself being
addressed in perfect English..." Well I'll be bound! By all the Gods
'tis an Englishman or I mistake my mark. I'll shake your hand sir
and tell you bluntly no man was ever more surprised than I at this
moment." William took his hand and laughed in sheer disbelief.

"Faith sir but you take my lines. I am William Wilkins of the
Missionary Society of London."

"Thomas Byrne at your service, late of His Majesty's Ship
Pandora. You are exceedingly welcome Mr. Wilkins and I insist you
accept my hospitality."

The poor missionary's dumbfounding was now complete. This
information sent him reeling and he was scarce able to gather his
wits. Those infamous events had taken place twenty years before he
was born, but like everyone in England he was intimately acquaint-
ed with the history of the Bounty and the terrible fate of the Pandora,
sent out to track down the mutineers.

"I promise you sir, your surprise cannot possibly exceed my own"
said William. "I accept your invitation with the greatest pleasure
but I beseech you sir, I must know your story." Thomas Byrne did
not answer him. Instead he turned to his canoe and invited the

preacher to assist him with his catch. Struggling to walk in the sand with a heavy basket of fish swung over his shoulder, William followed him up the beach but continued his plea in a most earnest fashion. "Mr Byrne sir I do beg of you, I must know your story for 'tis of the greatest interest to me."

"Well there is time enough for that" replied Thomas, "but come now, it is not far to my house and if you carry those fish you'll have earned your supper." He laughed out loud again. "In faith Mr Wilkins I am still greatly in shock. I had not expected to see an Englishman again. True I have heard stories about the preacher on Upolu but it has not been my good fortune to travel there. Once in a great while we sight a tall ship but they do not call here, this is a quiet place, there are no ports on Savai'i."

"I take it that you speak the native tongue Mr Byrne. Having lived here so long it could surely not be otherwise?"

"Why naturally Mr Wilkins, in practical ways it has become my first tongue but many years past. And you are correct, it could not have been otherwise. But in my learning of the tongue those natives with whom I lived acquired English from me in equal measure. It was a natural consequence, the one of the other. And I have raised my family here to be fluent speakers of English as well as their native tongue. I always considered it to be of the utmost importance."

"Your family you say?"

"Indeed Mr Wilkins, and you will meet them presently. Or I should say some of them. My son and his family have gone to another village to see a friend who is sick. But my daughter Eliza is here and will help her mother to cook supper for us and for her husband and children."

"Your family is large Mr Byrne?"

"It is the fa'a - the Samoan way of things, but no, my family is small by comparison with those of most natives."

"Eliza?"

"It was my mother's name. My wife is called Sisi. But begging your indulgence Mr Wilkins, I left England in my fourteenth year - 1790 it was - and fully expecting to see it again a year or so hence.

Here life is very simple, things do not change, but I can only wonder at what life would be in England now. I fear therefore you have an inordinate weight of news for me Mr.Wilkins and I await it's delivery with the keenest intention."

"Well then sir there is a deal of trading to be done. My transport of your catch in return for your hospitality, on that we are agreed, but my history for yours, now that is a more substantial transaction."

"It is indeed Mr Wilkins and one that I suspect a single evening will fail to accommodate."

*

The two men sat comfortably on a mat in Thomas Byrne's hut - or 'farlay' as he called it - smoking and digesting their excellent supper of steamed fish, pork and bananas. The children and women had withdrawn to other farlays, leaving them alone to jaw the night away. The place was very quiet and the air warm and sultry. Though the two men sat in silence there was an air of great expectation and a certain tension between them. William's curiosity was so keen that he was fit to burst, but at the same time he was sensible of the other's obvious reluctance to tell his story. For his part Thomas knew that he had no choice, that he could not deny the man his satisfaction. But he had not spoken of those events in forty-three years and had seldom even dwelt on them privately. He knew that he would not be able to account for himself without a measure of candour. But William was a man of the cloth and therefore of the utmost discretion, he was sure of that. Although they had known each other but a few hours he felt comfortable with William. Moreover, he had a sense that finally telling his tale after all these years might help him in some curious way, as though, while painful, it would be some sort of a relief for him.

It was William who broke the silence. "So Thomas, while I am yet to know the reason why the Pandora set you down here, I must assume that you are ignorant of the fate of that poor ship."

"The fate you say? I have always imagined she returned to England and saw the mutineers hanged, is that not so?"

"Not so at all. Indeed I have to tell you Thomas that your remaining on this island is perhaps a thing you should be mighty grateful for, as the tale of the Pandora is not much less extraordinary than that of the Bounty herself."

"Then I pray you William, don't keep it from me a moment longer. Tell me what happened."

"Well Thomas, the ship met a cruel end while attempting to make passage through Endeavour Straits. She foundered on a reef and was lost with many hands. But many also survived the wreck, including most of the prisoners, and continued in the ship's boats to reach the Dutch East Indies. They travelled not one third the distance covered by Captain Bligh, but for all it was a remarkable voyage - more than a thousand miles in open boats. Four of the mutineers were drowned in the wreck but the others were brought to England; several were pardoned and three of them hanged at the yard arm."

"Well William I am speechless. For all my sometime sorrow at not seeing England or my mother again it seems that had I stayed with the ship I might not have done so anyway. In faith William I am not sure how to receive this news. I am not sure how to feel about the matter at all."

"Would that I could counsel you Thomas, but I know nothing of the circumstances of your leaving the ship, or indeed anything else of your history. I am sensible that it clearly disturbs you to speak of these things but I beseech you Thomas, tell me what you can. You have my word as a man of God that your story will be received in the utmost confidence."

Thomas regarded his new friend with a stare that seemed to the preacher at once remote yet penetrating and he did so for some considerable time. At length though his body appeared to sink, as if in resignation; he looked to the floor for a moment then back at William with a different, easier expression. "Then it is time to tell it" he said, "you should make yourself comfortable William for it is a lengthy tale and, I warn you, in parts of a most base and unsavoury nature."

"Let me assure you Thomas, I myself was five months aboard a deep water navy ship and while I admit the greater part of my time at sea was not spent in the company of the common seamen, I can promise you that if my sensibilities were in any sort of a delicate nature before the voyage then they are now fully and most assuredly blunted."

"I'll take you at your word William, though I am affeared I may have shocks for you yet." Thomas adjusted his position on the woven mat slightly so as to be more comfortable, then he sat quietly for a moment, his eyes seeming to go somewhere far away.

"As a boy I lived in Hampshire. My pa was a farm labourer and we lived in a tied cottage on the estate. There was just the three of us, ma, pa and me. My pa was a stocky, thick-set man and possessed of a fiery temper. I can remember little else about him save that I didn't care for him much, but he took sick with the consumption and it did for him. I'd just about turned fourteen. My ma took it very bad. There was no work for her on the farm and we had to leave and seek parish relief at the workhouse in Winchester. 'Till that time I'd had the benefit of attending the village school and had learned properly to read and write. I loved school and I remember feeling that leaving there was worse than anything else that happened.

"But somehow my uncle Thomas got to hear of our plight and came to see us. He lived some miles away and up to that time I only knew him slightly. He arrived with the news that farm labouring was no life for him and he was journeying to Portsmouth to volunteer for service at sea. Moreover that he was of a mind to take me with him as my ma could not properly support me and it would be an excellent adventure and education for a young lad. He assured us that many children went to sea in navy ships, let alone young lads like me. Ma and I both thought it a capital idea and it was agreed there and then without much more talk.

"Uncle Thomas and I walked to Portsmouth. I remember it took us five days. Parting from ma had not been so sad as never in my dreams did I think that I would not see her again. We all thought to my being away for a year or so at most.

"Now this was the autumn of seventeen-ninety and all of England was talking about William Bligh and the amazing events on the Bounty. How they had lived as natives in the South Seas and then after, when the rigours of sea life got to be too much for them Fletcher Christian and a small band had seized the ship and cast Bligh and those loyal to him adrift in an open boat. How Bligh, against all the odds, had steered his little boat across more than three thousand miles of ocean to reach safety in the Dutch East Indies, thence returning to England to tell his tale. Bligh was a hero up and down the land, his story quite the most romantic of adventures and I could never have dreamed that I would ever go to these places let alone have anything to do with those events.

Uncle Thomas and I reached the top of Portsdown Hill and I saw the sea for the first time in my life. It was a bright shining plain of silver laying before the Isle of Wight and extending, to the side of the island into a misty, hazy eternity. We rested there awhile and I gazed at it, scarce able to take it in, much less to believe that I was really to venture out into that glassy nothingness.

On reaching Portsmouth we found lodgings at an inn where we quickly learned - indeed it was the talk of town - that a small frigate - the Pandora - was shortly to be dispatched to Tahiti charged with the task of apprehending the villains and returning them to England to face their punishment. Bligh had been of the opinion that following the mutiny they intended to return to Tahiti and there continue in their uncivilised ways. Uncle Thomas went to the offices of the Navy to volunteer us for service, never imagining that we would both end up in that ship. But the following morning a message came to the inn that we were to attend at the offices in Portsmouth dockyard. We duly made our way along and I remember that meeting William as though it had happened this very morning. A grey haired man informed us that the frigate Pandora was departing for a long voyage that would not see her back in English waters for a year or more. He handed my uncle some papers and instructed us to attend at the harbour and present ourselves to a Captain Edwards.

"My head spun at this news. Until a few weeks before I had never even been out of our little village and coming to Portsmouth was in itself an adventure for me. But then to find that I was to journey to the South Seas and there to have some involvement in this remarkable story was more than a poor lad could properly swallow.

"Our meeting with Edward Edwards brought me quickly back to myself though and with a cold bump. He was extremely tall and thin and had icy blue eyes. He stared down at me with a fierce expression. His face was white and bony. This was the first and almost the only time he ever spoke directly to me and I am at a loss to recall just what he said, but his voice and bearing left me in no doubt that our business was a serious one and that shipboard life would in no way be any sort of a recreation.

"My uncle was enlisted as an ordinary seaman, but I was not formally admitted to naval ranks. I found it was common for young men like myself to be taken aboard ships with no particular job to do. The idea was that by the time you came of age, that is if you had stuck with the life, you would be a seasoned and knowledgeable sailor and thereby of great use to the navy. So on the ship I was free to do much as I pleased and I am sure the navy thought it was fine for me to do so since I was sure to learn much about sailing and the ways of the ship just from being about. But I tell you William, the world I had entered could not have been more strange to me or more different from anything I had then experienced. The ordinary sailors wore clothes I had never seen before - funny breeches and half-coats - 'bum-freezers' they called them. And their language was often beyond my understanding - words and terms and sayings the like of which I had never heard. But more than that - the ship itself was very much like a little world of it's own. The Pandora was small by navy standards - a frigate of twenty-four guns with a hundred and sixty men aboard. I saw another in Portsmouth fairly twice the size, my uncle said it was a seventy-four gunner and would have had a crew of four hundred or more. I remember the ropes being cast off *and the ship being worked out into the Solent. It was as if a piece of England was breaking away and floating out to sea, and I with it. And yet as I say it was of itself another world, entirely and altogether strange.*

"Oh William it was so many years ago yet the things you remember, the things that stay with you. I recall some amazement at finding myself in a world of water - like to being in a dream it was. All about us was water as far as you could see and not a piece of land anywhere. I remember the movement of the ship, how it changed when we got out of coastal water and felt the big ocean swells; the pitching and rolling I quickly grew accustomed to, but it changed with different weather and under different sails. And the creaking - I hear that creaking still. Sometimes at night I'd lay and listen and it would seem that the ship must certainly tear apart. Uncle Thomas and I shared a hammock, slung from beams in the gun deck like all the others. He always worked daylight watches, not being then very experienced, and at night I slept with him. This was a bit strange at first but I quickly grew to like it, snuggled in there with his arm around me, all cosy and warm.

"We called in at Tenerife for provisions. Shortly after we found very calm weather and made little progress. It grew very hot and for a while I took to sleeping up on the deck at night. But a dreadful thing happened - Uncle Thomas took sick, I never knew what with, but he lay in the sick bay for several days and I was not allowed to see or go near him for fear that it was infectious. Early one morning one of the men woke me with the news that he had passed away in the night. The whole company was soon mustered and he was sent to the deep with a ceremony, all wrapped in white cloth. I watched him go into the water and disappear beneath, scarce able to believe what had happened, but feeling my last link with home was now severed and I was quite alone. It was forty-four years ago William but I remember it like it was yesterday - standing on that deck watching bubbles rise as my poor uncle went to the deep.

"For a day or two the wind left us completely and I did little but sit and stare at the water where my uncle had gone. When the wind at last freshened and the ship made way it was the hardest agony I

felt to leave the place. But the ship had her business to be about; she was carried by the wind and so I by her. I was a prisoner within her timbers and thereby at the mercy of the wind in her sails and I surrendered William. I gave up. I roamed the decks, speaking to noone and spent long hours in my hammock thinking of nothing but the smell of my uncle and the warmth of his body around me.

"The weather grew foul as we entered the Trade-winds and the ship tossed about like a thing of no substance. Everywhere was damp and cold as the spray was terrible over the decks and it got into all of the ship. All thoughts of our destination, or the adventure of our business were gone from me and with them any pleasure I might have taken or spirit to endure the trial. I withdrew completely to my bed, as miserable a lad as ever there was.

"It was in these conditions that we crossed the line and this was accompanied by much merrymaking in the ship's company. The tradition was for any novice sailors, or even midshipmen, to be swung over the side on ropes and given a thorough ducking. But the weather was so bad that Captain Edwards would not allow it. Instead the men were given extra rations of grog and danced and sang below decks in great spirits. I of course took no part in their celebrations but lay quietly in my sorry state.

"Dr Hamilton was the ship's surgeon and a kindly man. He came to see me, greatly concerned about my condition. It was his opinion that I was not ill but simply in need of some activity to bring me out of myself. My protests were very weak and he left, promising to arrange things. A little while later two seamen of the stockiest and most solid frames lifted me bodily from my hammock and carried me by the arms up to the forecastle. There I was met by Mr Oliver, who I knew to be the Master's Mate. He told me bluntly that moping and misery were no good for a lad and that it was time for my seaman's training to begin proper. He told me to climb the rigging of the foremast - just up and down to get the feel of it. I stood stockly before him, hardly able to believe he was serious in his demand, but he cuffed my ear amid a deal of abuse and this so shocked me that I leapt upon the rigging in a most lively fashion. But I didn't get more than a few steps up before I was taken with the *utmost fright and froze solid in my perilous position. The rolling of the ship straight away seemed much greater so that I needed all my strength just to hold on and I was certain I should be pitched into the deep at any moment. Mr Oliver soon realised the exercise was in vain and he ordered the two seamen to carry me off the ropes. They went about this with great ease and energy and accompanied their work with a deal of laughter. Back on the safety of the hard deck I felt greatly relieved and straight away burst into tears and wept inconsolably. Mr Oliver placed his hand on my head and pronounced me beyond help. I was sent below for hot mush and from then on left alone to my despair. Dr Hamilton continued to pay me attention though, making it his business to come and speak with me each day.*

*

Mark put his pen down and leaned back in the chair. He realised suddenly that he was cold. It was very quiet. He felt decidedly odd, as though he had woken abruptly from a dream and hadn't quite connected with the real world yet. He looked at his watch - it was one-thirty. For a moment he wasn't sure what this meant, then his mind focussed and he knew it was one-thirty in the morning and he had been writing without a break for over six hours. He had never experienced anything like it before - such a flood of concentrated inspiration - never before been so wrapped up in his writing that so much time could pass without him thinking for a moment about anything else. He hadn't even been to the loo. Now that he had stopped he felt very tired, his arms and legs were stiff and heavy as he stood and stretched. He walked leadenly up the stairs, cleaned his teeth, undressed and fell into bed. He was very satisfied with himself and, deep down, very excited. But he was far too tired to allow this excitement to break out, he just enjoyed feeling it there. He snuggled down contentedly under the duvet and in a few minutes was deeply asleep.

The next morning was Saturday and he slept until after ten. He lay in bed for a while, not really dozing, just putting off getting up. He knew he would have to read through his piece and was worried that, in the cold light of day, it would turn out to be complete rubbish. It would certainly not be the first time this had happened, but it would be a tragedy after such a protracted burst of inspiration. One or two things already occurred to him - if Thomas had left England at fourteen and lived exclusively with Polynesians for over forty years it was doubtful he would still speak English so fluently - or indeed that he would ever have been so articulate in the first place. He would more likely have spoken some sort of pidgin of his own, but it was beyond Mark's powers to try to emulate something like that and no reader would understand it anyway. So he allowed himself a measure of artistic licence - in any case he needed Thomas and William to be able to communicate easily straight away. And that was the other thing - the relationship between the two men would be more likely to develop over a much longer period of time before, as Mark was planning it, Thomas reached the point where he would feel able to disclose so tender a thing as the abuse he suffered. But he knew that lots of things in the story would change and develop as he worked on it; it was just a lump of clay he was throwing down last night and as yet he had no idea what it might turn into.

So he came downstairs in good spirits, picked the post up from the mat without looking closely at it, passed by the manuscript lying on the table and went into the kitchen. He always liked Saturday mornings - the relief of not feeling hurried, the sense of potential offered by the weekend ahead. Potential for what he was never quite sure, just the time to do what he wanted, to go at his own pace for a change. He would sit on a stool in the kitchen wearing only his boxer shorts, enjoy a plate of toast, a mug of coffee and a long, leisurely play with himself. Often in the mornings his willy would have a character that it didn't have at other times - heavy and full without actually being erect. The flesh then took on a firm but springy texture that he found completely irresistible. On weekdays he never had the time to enjoy it, but on Saturdays ... on Saturdays he could sit there and explore his private flesh to his heart's content. When at last he ejaculated, his semen would arc through the air and splatt on the kitchen floor and he always loved the feeling of this. It was a bit like pissing in the bath or eating messy food with your fingers - a momentary return to the glorious freedoms of childhood.

He mopped up his deposits, made another cup of coffee and looked at his mail. A credit card bill he left unopened, an invitation to take out private medical insurance went straight in the bin, but the third letter intrigued him. It was post-marked Cambridge with his name and address neatly typed and the envelope was of very high quality paper. He didn't know anyone in Cambridge now that Winifred had died. He opened the envelope. It was from a firm of solicitors - Hynard, Hynard and Ball of Trumpington Street:

Dear Mr Fletcher,
Enclosed please find our cheque in the sum of three thousand pounds, this being the amount bequeathed to you in the Will of our client Mrs Winifred Fletcher (deceased) from her estate. I would be most grateful if you could complete   the enclosed receipt and return it to us for our records.
Yours sincerely,
Martin Hynard   LL.B.

The exquisitely handwritten cheque was stapled to the bottom of the letter. Mark stared at it in utter astonishment. He had had absolutely no idea about this, none whatsoever. A warm glow rose inside him. 'Winifred you angel' he said out loud , 'you *angel*! I don't know where it is you've gone dear but you're smiling down on me, that's for sure.' Almost in the same instant he knew precisely what he would do with the money; it was mapped out in front of him as if he had opened a book and was looking straight at the pictures. He would go back to Sydney and spend some time with Phyllis, then on to Samoa - oh yes indeed - he would find out at first hand what Polynesia was really like and pay a visit to Stevenson's tomb.

The telephone rang. As usual he knew it was her.

"Oh hello dear, only me."

"Oh hello mother, how are you?"

"Yes, yes, musn't grumble. How are you dear?"

"Oh you know - muddling through. What can I do for you?"

"Mark isn't it wonderful? You must be thrilled to bits."

"Isn't what wonderful? What are you talking about?"

"The money of course, the money. Three thousand pounds eh? Who would have thought it?"

"Mother how on earth did you know? The cheque only came this morning. I've just this second opened it. What's going on?"

"I've spoken to Leonard, he told me all about it. She left three thousand to each of her grandchildren. Seems she was a bit of a dark horse your Nanna, none of us ever realised she had money like that stashed away. What do you think you'll do with it?"

"Oh mother for goodness sake I've just opened the envelope thirty seconds ago, I haven't even taken it in yet, how should I know what I'm going to do with it?" Thinking on his feet came naturally to Mark in situations like this. It was second nature for him to be guarded where his mother was concerned. He had had years of practice at it and now automatically gave the minimum of information - or no information at all - until he had had a chance to consider the implications of her knowing whatever it was. In this case she would be very upset to learn that he intended to travel to Australia and spend time with Phyllis again. He had also quickly realised that in all probability it would be several months, perhaps longer, before a trip like that could be organised and she would spend the whole time being deeply irritating about it.

The two women had disliked each other for years. They had been at school together, along with Mark's father and his brother Bill, and some feud or mutual resentment which Mark had never got to the bottom of, not that he cared much, went all the way back to their teenage years. His parents had been childhood sweethearts and married in their early twenties. Angela had evidently been horrified when Bill - her own brother-in-law - began dating, then married, the dreaded Phyllis and Mark could still remember his mother's undisguised satisfaction when they announced they were to emigrate to Australia. At the age of ten he didn't understand what her animosity was about, and he still didn't. From time to time, over the years, he had tried to weedle it out of her but she had remained resolutely tight-lipped on the subject, as indeed had Phyllis, to his surprise, when he had asked her (rather more bluntly than he had his mother).

But when he returned from living in Australia he had been unable to hide the fact that he and Phyllis had got on like a house on fire and his poor mother had been stricken with the keenest jealousy. She told herself it was just her paranoia, but she couldn't help suspecting - correctly as it turned out - that Phyllis had the sort of relationship with Mark that she pretended to herself she had, although knowing really that she didn't. That they talked to each other - actually communicated about personal issues. She couldn't bear to think of it really, but she did - often - torturing herself with thoughts of the bond she knew existed between them, the bond that should have been hers - by right - she was his mother for God's sake! But what she and Mark had was a veneer, a smooth surface with no substance to it. And of all people it had to be Phyllis who held a key - who found a way in - who had robbed her of the one thing she wanted more than anything else and didn't know how to get.

Mark was very sanguine about it all and in any case didn't really understand the full extent of his mother's angst, but he knew it was a tender area and instinctively avoided it, unless of course he was particularly cross with her about something when he might use it to have a small though admittedly cruel dig. So today he didn't tell her anything about his plans, such as they were, that could wait until much nearer the time. He made small-talk for a few minutes then got her off the phone on the pretext that he needed to go shopping. He looked at the time, it was eleven-thirty; nine-thirty in the evening in Sydney, not too late for Bill and Phyl by any means, but he decided to give the whole matter some thought and then ring them in the evening. He made another cup of coffee, gathered himself and returned to his manuscript.

*

"*Some weeks later we found ourselves once more becalmed. For many days the blow had been constantly from the east and the ship had barrelled along downwind under full sail, rolling steadily from side to side. That rolling had been so constant that I had almost ceased to notice it and when the wind at last went round to the north, then dropped away altogether it felt mighty strange to be level again and for a day or two I was right seasick. By now I was up and about the decks a bit more and feeling something like my old self again, though I missed Uncle Thomas dreadfully and still did not mix much with the men. And by and large they also left me to myself. Their talk and their ways always remained strange to me, like as they were not Englishmen at all but were come instead from some foreign part. But one particular man did become something of a friend - it started soon after we had found ourselves becalmed as I have said.*

"*Some of the men were fishing and I was watching them with interest. They trailed lines over the side hooked with small bits of salt pork from their ration. After a time a big grey shape came up*

under the ship and swam by, twice the size of any man. 'Look live-
ly now lads' - said one of the group - 'it's a shark, a fine one and no
mistake.'

"What's a shark?" I said, so curious about the creature that I'd
forgotten myself and it was only after that I wondered at my behaviour, striking up like that. One of the men answered me, saying that
a shark was a big fish and a nasty bugger too that would eat any
man who tried to swim with him, but if we could catch one it would
make mighty good eating and a welcome change from navy rations.
With that the great fish came alongside once more and took one of
the baits. A cheer went up and the men jumped and hauled together on the line. The beast was thrashing about in the water and
struggling mightily but there were six men pulling and they soon had
him up over the bulwarks and onto the deck where he continued to
thrash about, knocking one man clean off his feet.

"The fellow who'd spoken to me made a motion with his arm to
keep me clear of the thing. Another came running with a big mallet
and landed the fish a mighty blow square on it's head. Still it wriggled, though much less than before, but the men all set on it at once
with their knives and in a minute or two the poor thing was no
longer a fish at all but a pile of thick steaks. The long backbone and
the head and tail were tossed back into the sea. The men divided out
their shares, washed down the deck and went off to see the cook.

Sometime later the man who had spoken to me and then sought
to protect me from the shark's tail came up on deck and approached
me. He carried a great lump of white meat on a platter and asked if
I felt like sharing it. I'll tell you William I didn't need to be asked
twice; growing up on a farm I had always been lucky to have a good
variety of foods and the salt beef and hard bread the Navy offered
day after day was hard to endure. This was a feast and no mistake
so I thanked him kindly and ate my share with a deal of pleasure.

"He told me his name was Harry Lamb and that he was sorry
about my uncle. He said that Dr Hamilton had no idea what ail-
ment had taken him and that the whole company had been much
affeared that it would spread over the ship. He said the men had

avoided me as they thought I might be carrying it, seeing as how the two of us had shared a hammock. But now it was a month or more since he died and no-one else had taken sick, people were starting to forget about it. He pointed out to sea and said that two days' sailing that way - if but we had some wind - would bring us onto the coast of Brazil. I'd never heard of it before. He talked of thick green jungles and swamps and mosquitos and I stared across the flat sea, trying to picture the place.

"From that time on Harry took me into his care a bit. He would come and find me after he came off watch and we would sup together. Then he would show me how to tie knots or teach me about the workings of the ship - how to read what the weather was doing - what the different sails were for - all sorts of things. I can't remember much of it now, but it was mighty interesting at the time and I started to think less about my uncle and to take more notice of the life of the ship.

"The weather grew foul as we got further south in the weeks ahead and we were all issued with warmer clothing - thick woollen shirts and breeches. My new friendship with Harry made things easier to bear, but it was a dismal time of heavy grey seas, cold, damp and the endless pitching and creaking of the ship. One morning Harry came and told me that we had passed the line of Cape Horn during the night, though we were some way off to the south and there was no land to be seen, and that we were now coming into the wide Pacific which meant the weather would at last start to cheer up. And he was right. With each passing day it grew slowly warmer and all our spirits lifted. But we had been at sea for four months and I had begun to wonder if we would ever see land again. One day, when I was stood gazing out at the endless ocean, a sailor came up to me and said that you could go a thousand miles in any direction you pleased and find nothing but sea. One of the officers happened by and on hearing him said this wasn't wholly true - that a day's sail to the north lay a small rock called Pitcairn's Island, but as no-one lived there and we were only two weeks from Tahiti with plenty of provisions remaining there was no call for us to visit it."

William sat up at this news and his first thought was to interrupt his friend. But Thomas was lost in his story and he decided it would serve no purpose at this point to enlighten him about Pitcairn's Island. 'But my word!' he thought 'if only they had known that this was precisely where Fletcher Christian and his party had washed up.'

"We sighted Tahiti about three weeks later, in fact I remember it was the twenty-second of March 1791. The shout went up from high in the rigging. One of the officers called 'Where-away?' 'Five degrees on the port bow' came the reply. Well, excitement spread over the ship like a crop fire with the wind under it. Crowds of men leaping into the rigging or cramming the rail and straining for a first glimpse, cheering, waving and dancing on the decks. Someone fired a musket into the air - one of the officers - and the men were brought to order and those on watch sent about their proper business. But the general feeling of relief was something to behold.

"I made my way up to the bows and peered ahead. There it was, unmistakeable, a small grey thing, far off in the hazy distance, but solid. I hardly took my eyes from it all day but stood there in the bows of the ship, scarce able to believe I was actually staring at a real South Sea island. As the hours passed and we slowly drew nearer the craggy line of the hills became more distinct and the colour filled to a dark green. I was entranced. At five miles off we hove-to. They said the airs were too light and we couldn't get near enough to work the ship into the anchorage in daylight. So we passed a terrible night. The men were desperate to get ashore after so long at sea and talked of nothing but native women who wore no clothes and how the place was truly paradise.

"At first light a freshening breeze allowed us to work up to Matavai Bay, where the Bounty had lain throughout her months here, and where we were to drop anchor. But before we ever reached the anchorage a small canoe came towards us, paddled with great energy by three native men - my first sight of a real Tahitian. We altered course a bit and they came alongside - clearly being highly skilled at handling their little craft. A rope was thrown and two of them climbed aboard. They were brown as berries, dressed only in loincloths and covered richly in tattoos.

"Most of us on the ship had never seen such men and we crowded round them, pushing and shoving to get a better look. But none of us were at all prepared for what happened next. I imagine William that your surprise when we encountered each other this afternoon must have been something akin to what I, and indeed all of the ship's company, felt at that moment for - to the astonishment of all about - one of them addressed us in the King's English, saying he was Peter Heywood, late Midshipman of His Majesty's Ship Bounty and that he would be happy to pilot us into the anchorage. Well, the entire ship's company fell silent at this and I believe a puff of wind would have knocked us all down. A guard of Marines was straight away summoned and the man - with a look of astonishment on his face that was equal to our own - was marched off to the quarter-deck and presented to Captain Edwards. We could see, on a closer look, that he was indeed not a native, despite his brown skin, and we took it therefore that he was one of the mutineers. But if this was so then it puzzled me that he should have jumped onto the ship in so lively a fashion and presented himself so openly. Captain Edwards gave him a deal of abuse, at which the man was sorely offended and he protested his innocence most earnestly. But Edwards would have none of it and the man was handcuffed and taken into the Captain's cabin - we supposed for further questioning.

After the ship had anchored a number of canoes came out to us and the natives climbed aboard. Mostly they were taller than us and well-made, handsome people. But they wore so little, just loincloths or wrapped-around skirts, and they were so happy and so unashamed. The women all displayed their breasts with no sign of modesty or shyness and the response of the men was something to behold. They laughed and danced, some even cried, and nearly all of them had their eyes so wide I thought they might pop right out of their heads. I had never seen grown men - and tough old sea-dogs at that - acting so silly and this was nearly as strange to me as all the naked flesh round about. The commotion on the deck was something to behold.

"Three more Englishmen came aboard, each every bit as willingly it seemed as Heywood had done. I don't recall their names, but one was dressed in what remained of a midshipman's uniform and the others in ragged clothes. They all protested their innocence in the mutiny but were nevertheless clapped into irons and taken below. All the talk of the ship was about whether these four were really mutineers or not. Some said there had not been room in Bligh's launch for all the loyal men and several had therefore been forced to remain in the Bounty against their will. If this were so it would account for these men's protests, but this would also have been a good scheme for getting away with it. They must have known the Admiralty had a mighty long arm and would one day come for them and they'd had nigh on two years to come up with a story.

"One of our lieutenants was a Thomas Heywood who had sailed on the Bounty as a midshipman and gone with Bligh in the launch. Since he had actually been present at the mutiny he could have told us everything, but he was a tight-lipped and surly bugger who refused ever to discuss the matter. I remember him being called to the Captain's cabin soon after the first bloke came on board and was taken there. He came out again very quickly and looking grim-faced, but he wouldn't say a word to anyone. There was even talk that they might have been brothers - seeing as they had the same name.

"So the business of the ship was gone about. Parties were dispatched ashore with gifts for the natives and to secure provisions. I was allowed to go in one of the boats and well remember my surprise at jumping off and finding how warm the water was after all the months of cold sea-spray over the decks. Indeed it amuses me now to think back and recall how strange everything seemed - the blueness of the water, the dark green of the forest, the startling white of the beach, the brilliance and great size of the flowers, the huts with their domed roofs of thatch, the naked people, the little hogs running everywhere. It's all been my world for so many years now, but to think back - can you imagine William how it all seemed to a lad of

*fifteen, as I was by then, who's never been out of his Hampshire vil-
lage 'till six months before? But I'm boring you William - you want
to know how it was I came to remain in this place and I'm spinning
my yarn out with such details as I'm sure don't command your interest."*

*William hadn't spoken in over an hour and it now seemed
wrong to do so - as if it would break the spell that Thomas had cast.
So he held up his hands to show that his friend was far from correct
and gestured that he was more than happy for him to continue.*

*"It became known that several of the mutineers had succeeded
in constructing a small vessel in which they had made off for another island, thereby seeking to evade capture. A launch was dispatched
and presently returned with three of the fellows and a splendid
schooner in tow. It was thirty-five feet in length, I recall, and such
a handsome craft that we could scarce believe these men had fashioned it from a few felled trees and with only primitive tools to hand.
They had named her the Resolution, which seemed an appropriate
name in the circumstances. Some days later seven more men were
brought from this same island, making fourteen prisoners in all, but
Fletcher Christian was not among them and for Captain Edwards
this was cause for the deepest frustration.*

*"I only learned what I could from the talk amongst the men, but
it seemed that following the mutiny, which took place a great distance away in the Friendly Islands, Christian had returned to Tahiti
and set sixteen men down, that having been their choice. That two
of these had afterwards died, hence our fourteen prisoners, and he
had then returned to sea with a band of eight mutineers and a number of natives. His plan, as far as anyone knew, had been to find
some unknown island where the Admiralty might not search, run the
ship aground and use her timbers to build a settlement. And so they
had disappeared into the great Pacific and had not been heard of
since.*

*"We only remained two weeks at Matavai Bay. Captain
Edwards had learned all he could about Christian and was impa-
tient to be after his quarry. During our stay in Tahiti Dr Hamilton*

had protested about the foul conditions in which the prisoners were held and so a makeshift cabin was erected on the quarter-deck. Being of a rounded construction it was at first referred to as 'the Round-house', but before long someone came up with 'Pandora's Box' and this was the name that stuck. All fourteen prisoners were kept in there, shackled to the floor with heavy chains.

Thomas paused for a moment and stared at the floor with a serious expression. "My tale becomes darker now William" he said, "... and I might say more painful to tell. I have not spoken of these things in forty-four years and though I confess I have dwelt on them from time to time, I have not succeeded in making too much sense of what happened. My hope is that as long as you have the stomach to hear it then as a learned man you might perhaps offer me some guidance." William did not answer, but in an effort to reassure he smiled warmly at his friend and nodded slowly.

Five

"Phyl!"

"Oh Christ! Who the bloody hell's ringing me at seven in the morning?"

"Don't give me that. If I know you you've mowed the lawn, vacuumed the house, cleaned the windows, run three miles on the beach and you're just finishing your seventh cup of coffee."

"Eighth actually, ha ha ha ha ... how are you darling? This is a nice surprise."

"I'm fine Phyl, really fine. What about you?"

"Oh ... growing old."

"Phyllis you'll never grow old."

"Is that right? So anyway come on, have you met any nice men lately?"

"No, afraid not."

"Well what the hell are you ringing me for if you haven't got any news?"

"I have got some news."

"Oh yeah? ... Go on then, thrill me."

"I'm coming to see you."

"Oh Jesus! And what did I do to deserve that?"

"You love me really."

"So what's brought this on? Oh let me guess ... nothing to do with Winifred's three grand I suppose?"

"How the hell did you know?"

"A-ha! We might be stuck out here in the colonies darling but we have our easr to the ground don't you worry. We don't miss much."

"But I only knew about it this morning!"

"Oh you know ... Bill and Leonard, they're always on the phone."

"I don't believe it ... nothing's sacred in this bloody family. My mother rang thirty seconds after I'd opened the letter and asked me what I was going to spend the money on."

"Now there's a surprise. You didn't tell her?"

"No of course I didn't tell her. Anyway ... aren't you excited?"

"What ... about you coming?"

"No, about Ireland winning the Eurovision Song Contest."

"Oh delirious. So when's the great event?"

"I don't know, depends when I can sort out enough time off work. Probably later in the year, around October-November time, how does that sound?"

"Fine, we never go anywhere."

"I'll probably only stay a week or so, then I'm off to Samoa."

"Samoa? What the hell for?"

"Why the hell not? The world is out there waiting to be explored Phyllis."

"Yeah right! And what's the real reason?"

"I just want to visit Polynesia, I want to see what it's like."

"Well it's hot. That's about it. Hot and humid. Bill had to go a couple of years back – something to do with coconut cream I think – an he hated it."

"Well the thing is ... I've been really interested in Robert Louis Stevenson – you know – the writer...?"

"Yes darling, belive it or not I have heard of him."

"Well he was ill you see, he had tuberculosis. He couldn't handle the climate at home. He went all the way to the South Pacific looking for somewhere he could breathe and Samoa was it. So I'm just interested that's all. I want to see what Samoa is like and I want to visit his tomb. If that's okay with you?"

"Ah ... now I understand."

"Now you understand what Phyllis?"

"It's not the same you know, it's not the same thing at all."

"Phyllis - what the fuck are you talking about?"

"Being gay Mark ... it's not a disease."

"I'm sorry? ... Run that by me again."

"You think you have to get twelve thousand miles away from England before you can relax enough to actually shag someone. Don't get me wrong, I hope you do – you never know – some nice friendly Samoan boy ... but it's not the answer darling."

Mark was momentarily stumped for words. "...Phyllis I haven't got the faintest idea what you are talking about."

"Oh yes you have. You know exactly what I'm talking about."

"Well anyway, this call's costing me a fortune."

"Yeah, bugger off and let me get on with Bill's breakfast. Ring me nearer the time and let me know about flights and stuff."

"Okay, and I'll reverse the charges next time."

"Piss off!"

"Love ya." He blew a kiss down the phone.

"Creep" she said and hung up.

*

As Mark took his seat on the plane he was pleased to find himself just forward of the wing. This was always his favourite position for it not only allowed a good view of the engines but he could also see straight down without the wing being in the way. He thought about the aircraft that had brought him all the way out here two weeks before. A spanking new jumbo jet, pristine and squeaky clean, it had climbed out from a dank and chilly London, crossed the North Sea, then the Baltic, then passed the night chugging across the vastness of Russia. Dawn found them surfing the jet-stream over the mountains of the Hindu Kush. The plains of northern India had thrown up a blaze of light and a riot of bumpy air, but then they had sailed smoothly across the

Indian Ocean, run down the Straits of Malacca and returned to earth at Singapore.

After a second short night and a remarkably red dawn they had hurtled across the desert that is most of Australia before at last sinking into the lush brilliance of a spring morning in Sydney.

Singapore had been their only stop in the whole, enormous journey. From one side of the world to the other and only touching the ground once! Any machine capable of such a feat deserved more than mere admiration as far as Mark was concerned; reverence came nearer, but he could never adequately articulate his feelings about the 747. What had saddened him in this instance was how the owners and operators of this fabulous craft could so horribly misunderstand it's true purpose. They had desecrated it, in Mark's view, with a smart, business-like, grey and blue decor that wasn't just inappropriate, it was downright antithetical in it's drab seriousness. The cabin attendants were models of sobriety. Power-dressed as though in readiness for a board meeting, they had set about their work like sensible Scottish nannies and the whole effect had conspired efficiently to outlaw any silly notion that air travel could possibly be an adventurous or romantic activity.

But that idea had found a glorious embodiment in this lovely, creaky old crate. Flown as it was by a company from a tropical climate, this aircraft sang a very different song. It had come from a wonderful place, somewhere out there in the ocean and like a messenger, an angel from Eden, it had come to collect him, to take him there. And he could already sense the place, could feel it's breath in the dazzling chroma that swathed the aircraft. Even now it was embracing him, drawing him in; and he was a helpless and happy prisoner, limp with pleasure and the most unbearable anticipation.

They tore down the runway, vibrating furiously and clawed their way into the air; then all was suddenly calm and quiet as they climbed out over Botany Bay and sail boats shrank to dots beneath them. The sand dunes of Kurnell, where Captain

Cook had anchored, and the great sweep of Cronulla beach all fell away far below as they struck out over the ocean. The seat belt sign went off with a familiar beep which was accompanied by a general stirring and unclinking of belts. Mark had held on to his pre-take-off pineapple juice and he sipped it now, watching the smudge of Australia slide away over the horizon as they rose, majestically like astronauts into a shining, silvery-blue void.

Adopting his usual position, face pressed against the window, Mark tried to concentrate on nothing but his wonderful suspension above the Earth. There was nothing to see, absolutely nothing, except blueness. The ocean, so far below, was deeply blue; the sky likewise, but in the distance they shaded to a hazy white and merged imperceptibly, offering no horizon for reference. It seemed to Mark that the plane was just hanging there in a great blue nothingness.

After several hours it grew dark - very dark indeed - and it happened very rapidly. He appreciated that it would be thus, given the latitude they were in and their distance - at least two thousand miles - from the nearest city. But he had been staring at space for so long it was easy to believe that he was now in it - floating peacefully off towards the asteroids, a tin can full of lost souls. The American pilot's nonchalant, clinical voice did nothing to reassure: sounding like no-one so much as a NASA technician speaking to the crew of Apollo 14, he helpfully announced that they were on 'a five mile final' and that the weather was 'scattered at seventeen hundred' - taking it for granted that his passengers understood what the hell he was on about. Mark scanned for signs of anything terrestrial, a light perhaps, but there was nothing out there to reassure - nothing at all - just inky, impenetrable blackness.

There is a precise moment in every flight, a moment that never failed to give him a small but acute thrill, when he would feel the aircraft begin to sink slightly. Often the movement was so slight as to be almost imperceptible, but it was tangible evidence that the destination was approaching and that arrival was therefore imminent. But while he felt that familiar little buzz, the motion of the plane now seemed strangely pointless - pointless to have any directional purpose in the midst of all this space. But it was also a hopeful sign. The Pacific Ocean spans half the planet and Mark was beginning to understand the true scale of it. The squiggle of volcanic rock they were aiming for was only a few square miles in size but the steady sinking of the plane was a reassurance that they must have found it okay. Nevertheless it was a shock when runway lights suddenly flared beneath him as he could still see absolutely nothing else, and stranger still to feel concrete under the wheels.

Stepping through the door of the aircraft he found himself immersed in warm, wet, spicy air. So incongruous in the middle of the night, it filled his lungs, infusing him with pleasure and forcing him to accept the reality that he had indeed arrived in a different part of the world. Although coming now from Australia the physical shock was not as great as it might have been, the air had a lovely, waxy quality that he had not experienced before. And as he walked away from the plane a pervasive rose-like scent oozed from the frangipani bushes that lined the path to the terminal, at first mingling with the smell of aviation fuel, then banishing all traces of it from his nostrils.

And so Mark had arrived in Pago Pago, capital of American Samoa. Not his final destination this, but airline timetables had dictated that he spend two nights here and so it was to be the site of his introduction to Polynesia.

The passengers formed a straggling line, shuffling wearily towards the airport buildings. For most this was nothing more than an inconvenient refuelling stop on the way up to Honolulu, but as they passed a small sign pointing to the arrivals hall a few individuals veered off in that direction, watched for the most part with vague bewilderment by the others. Mark turned towards the arrivals building and was confronted by a roof and some pillars to hold it up, but nothing resembling a wall anywhere. And something else wasn't right: something fundamental was definitely awry but he couldn't quite grasp what it was. He considered the night heat and the dampness, but that wasn't it. He flashed on the recollection of being in a vivid dream and realising he was dreaming. Then he knew, and the little slip from half to full consciousness of a thing was amazing to him. The whole place was completely, deeply silent. Individual sounds occurred around him, but appeared in sharp relief against a background of silence that seemed elemental - a stillness laying about him like a thick mist, tangible and infinite.

A man in a white shirt and blue sarong checked his passport disinterestedly, stamped it and waved him through into an area where a number of immensely fat Polynesians, all wearing sarongs, tee-shirts and flip-flops, were draped lethargically over benches. Perhaps this was a dream. Perhaps he would wake up to a chill morning in Essex and a quick pang of nostalgia. But no - this time he knew he would stay asleep long enough to find out what would happen. England was a million miles away and getting further by the minute. Even Phyllis was receding and he now felt disconnected from her, from everyone, as though he had crossed over into some other world.

Reaching the far side of the building he stood and stared into a wall of absolute darkness. The lights from the arrivals hall penetrated a few yards, but beyond that there was nothing. An enormous, bare-footed Samoan wearing a floral sarong of the most jarring colours appeared at his side from nowhere, muttered something about a taxi and in one graceful movement swept his bags up and floated away. A moment's hesitation and he knew he would certainly have lost the man to the cloying darkness and so, in a sudden wave of empathy with novice parachutists, he stepped off the edge.

He would much rather have arrived by sea. That had been his dream - to drift across an expanse of ocean for days, weeks, even months on end, eventually to see a distant grey smudge become a wooded hill, and finally a place. To have smelt earth and found it strange. To encounter a place, real but alien, exotic, full of new sounds and smells and colours. To have felt the distance mile by mile, and at last to have come in from the sea and rejoined the world of men, albeit in such an isolated place. But this landfall had not been a bad substitute and he was not about to complain. He had floated for hours through space - first blue then black - to arrive ... where? In map terms he knew, but where was he really? He had read much about Polynesia and had developed detailed imaginings, but his first actual experience here was of an impenetrable, smothering blanket of silence. Silence and darkness, dampness and heat - simple things but intense and intensely present, they disorientated him and yet somehow were immensely and curiously satisfying.

He sat in the taxi - a very old car of indeterminate origin - and they moved off. The dial never went above fifteen miles an hour and it was only rarely that they achieved even that speed. This stately progress ought to have maddened him, but the headlights made little impression on the oceanic night and for this reason alone he would have been comfortable. But the pace also seemed somehow appropriate, deferential, easing carefully along so as not to disturb the spell. The driver appeared to be in some sort of trance - his eyes were fixed on what he could see of the road ahead and his face was testament to a deep inner serenity. Mark could not draw him into conversation and his attempts to do so quickly felt out of place. So he just sat quietly.

Silence - darkness - dampness - heat. The fifth presence now was the ocean. He could not see it, but he could hear it - the rush of surf over the reef somewhere in the distance off to his right. It was a faint sound but a present one, and more than that he could smell it - salt and seaweed - the warm breath of a sleeping giant.

Entering the lobby of the Rainmaker Hotel Mark found himself in a cathedral space. An immense vaulted ceiling soared, perhaps sixty feet above him and the pervading, persistent silence lay all around. A tall, thin young Samoan showed him to his room. He couldn't help noticing how smooth and fluid the man's movements were - almost balletic. The taxi driver, though a large man, had moved in the same way. Then he remembered that he hadn't given the driver a tip, he hadn't thought of it, but now that he had a flicker of panic niggled him. What was the custom here? He didn't know. Would a tip be an expectation or an insult? The moment arrived as they entered the room and the young man placed his bags on the bed. Unable to decide on one course or the other he asked the Samoan what was usual. As the words came out of his mouth he squirmed inside, but the young man was very good. Sparing him any eye contact he bowed slightly and said "that is up to you sir." Mark held out a two dollar bill, the man took it and, bowing deeply, appeared to slide out of the room.

When he woke in the morning he lay for a while, re-running the previous day's events before opening his eyes. Then, confronted with the same room he remembered, but certain he was awake, he struggled a little to grasp the reality of his situation. He tried to picture the globe - looking square on at the Pacific he could only just see the continents around it's edge. Hawaii was a speck, plum in the middle, and if he moved south about half way down and a bit to the left, that was where he was sitting - right now - he really was. Three hundred miles south of here, in Tonga, was the spot where Fletcher Christian had seized the *Bounty*. About the same distance west was Fiji. Tahiti lay to the east, fifteen hundred miles of water between.

He took a shower, pulled on some shorts and a tee-shirt, drew back the curtains, opened the door and wandered out onto the lawn. What he saw stopped him dead in his tracks. Across the bay, not more than a mile or so away stood a mountain, two thousand feet high and coated from top to bottom in a thick mantle of vegetation. Buildings dotted around the water's edge looked like white hem stitching on a dark green curtain. Looking around he found himself surrounded by craggy peaks, each as lushly vegetated. The hotel lay on a spit of land half way along the bay, and the bay itself was a deep cleft, a sea cave, all but cutting the island in two.

The sky was a uniform slate-grey but it was hot nevertheless and Mark was in no doubt that it had rained during the night. Apart from the ground being obviously soaking, the air was so dense that he felt himself to be wading through it rather than walking. Looking along the bay he could see that Pago Pago was little more than a shanty town. Constrained by the geography, it lay strung out along a mile or so of waterfront while the cliffs of dark vegetation loomed above. As he walked along he quickly came to notice the tropical plants around him. The variety was tremendous, apart from the many coconut palms none were familiar to him but all of them possessed gigantic leaves and an imposing physical presence. The little town appeared to be a human toe-hold in imminent danger of vegetable inundation. He felt the rain forest would only have to breathe in in order effortlessly to reclaim it's waterfront and that it might indeed choose to do so at any moment.

He wandered through the town, almost floating in the hot, soggy air, engulfed by greenery and a darkly lowering sky and unnerved by the bottomless background of silence. Stranger still, yesterday had been Friday and today it was Friday again for he had crossed the International Dateline. For all he knew he had, like some latter-day Alice, slipped through the looking glass and landed a hundred years ago in the scene of a Joseph Conrad novel. Nor was he alone in making this transition, several Toyota four by fours had somehow arrived here too. But no-one seemed to take much notice of these incongruous machines - perhaps they were used to bits and pieces dropping through from the real world.

He was beginning to sense that the natural laws he was

accustomed to never obtained in this place, and though he needed no more evidence for this it was about to be provided anyway. Quite suddenly and with no warning that he had been aware of, the street emptied of people. They scuttled away and vanished like so many sand crabs under the nearest shelter, responding with apparent mass-consciousness to some unseen signal. At least, it was unseen to him - he had no idea what was happening, but he did not have to wait long to find out. To say that it started raining does no justice to what next occurred - St Peter opened a heavenly sluice gate and unleashed an instant downpour of biblical proportions. The buildings themselves quickly faded from view behind sheets - curtains of water. Mark stood under a waterfall, amazed not only that it was happening but that the water was so warm. But within minutes it stopped, as abruptly as it had started and exactly as if some great cosmic tap had been turned off. People emerged from their burrows and resumed their business as if nothing had happened, while he stood motionless amongst them, dazed and waterlogged, clutching his dripping camera. He felt like a child who had fallen in a pond.

Slopping his way back to the hotel he began to reflect on his Polynesian baptism. The weather was certainly depressing, but only in an abstract sort of way. There was a feeling of melancholia in the place, but he felt somehow shielded from it - protected by his excitement, his child-like sense of wonder at the place and his simple astonishment at finding himself here at all. More than that, a delicious and continuing anticipation bubbled away inside him. For all it's strangeness he was sure this was not the real Polynesia, that still awaited him across the sea. Instead it felt to him like a half-way house, a waiting station where you prepared and gathered yourself before stepping off the edge of the world.

Later that day he sat basking by the hotel pool in ninety degree heat under a dense black cloud that threatened to make the pool redundant at any moment. Some distance away in the grounds a rehearsal was taking place for some sort of fashion show or cabaret. Statuesque Polynesian women flounced about a makeshift stage watched by the hotel staff who were, for the most part, convulsed with laughter. From that distance he could not tell what was so funny so he wandered over. One of the performers moved exquisitely across to intercept him and enquired bluntly if he would be at the hotel the following night. They were having a fashion show, she said, and it would be lovely if he could come. Her long eyelashes moved lugubriously over beautiful, shiny eyes. He realised at once that she was a man. "Sorry" he said politely, "I'm leaving the island tomorrow." She shrugged her shoulders. "Pity" she said, and sauntered off. He watched her go. "But I'm here tonight." Somewhere at the back of his mind that was what he had wanted to say. But he watched her go, watched her bum swish as she strutted across the lawn. Then he made his way back to the pool, angry with himself for not being more adventurous but knowing that it would always be thus.

Six

At the airport early the next morning Mark sat and listened to the ocean surging on the reef. Though faint and distant it was the only sound. There were no aircraft to be seen and he wondered idly what sort of conveyance Polynesian Airlines would provide for the half-hour flight. The chain of islands that makes up Samoa is split politically – the small American group in the east, the larger group lying about seventy miles to the west and comprising one of the tiniest nations on earth – Western Samoa. Here on the island of 'Upolu is the capital – Apia – where Stevenson had lived out the last five years of his life and where Mark was presently headed.

His curiosity about the aircraft was relieved by the appearance, out of a lowering sky, of a DeHavilland Twin Otter. A substantial enough craft, he thought, with two splendidly noisy engines driving whirring propellers and, slung beneath the wings, a cabin whose huge picture windows held the promise of wonderful views. He clambered aboard along with ten or twelve Samoans, all wearing sarongs and tee-shirts, and was disappointed not to see any goats or chickens, feeling their presence would have been somehow appropriate. They bumped and clattered their way down the runway, heaved themselves off the ground with willpower and banked sharply for a low pass over the island.

He had been hoping for a glimpse of the tiny and remote islands of the Manu'a group where the anthropologist Margaret Mead had researched her famous book *Coming of Age in Samoa*. They were probably much too distant, but in any case the Australian pilot raised the nose and headed for the cloud base. Within seconds they were clenched by impenetrable dirty milk and for half an hour they pitched, rolled and banged their way along, occasionally catching dizzying glimpses of the ocean far below as they vaulted between banks of cloud. At one point cockpit door flew open and he could see the pilot wrestling manfully with the pedals and joy-stick – real seat-of –the-pants stuff. He pictured his mother opening the Daily Telegraph – 'Light plane lost in South Pacific – Briton thought to be among the passengers...'

Eventually they were all granted a measure of relief as the little plane swung out from under the clouds, finding clear air and the reward for their endurance which was the most spectacular of views. They were directly above the island of 'Upolu and could see beaches and lagoons on both sides of the aircraft. 'Upolu is long and narrow. It has a jagged backbone of extinct volcanoes and is completely covered in a thick mantle of vegetation. Every glance at the map revealed enchanted place names – Mulivai Beach, Toamua, Ti'avea, Malae-malu – he uttered them quietly and they rolled in his mouth like pieces of tropical fruit.

They flew up the length of the island, sinking steadily towards the tree tops, whistled low over a banana plantation and made a dignified landing at Faleolo International Airport. Not quite as grand a place as it sounded, it was nevertheless more recognisable as an airport than the one they had just left, though not for the presence of aircraft. Theirs was the only one in attendance and stepping out of it felt rather like opening an oven door while wrapped in a wet cloth.

He left the customs area and was greeted by a gaggle of taxi drivers – huge nut-brown men in sarongs, all anxious for a fare yet submitting themselves respectfully to his selection. He found this greatly embarrassing and, feeling for a moment like some colonial master choosing a slave, quickly picked the nearest one. "Thank you, thank you sir" said the man, bowing deeply. "I am Sam, I give you good ride you see. Thank you, thank you." He gathered up Mark's bags and strutted imperiously in front of his colleagues for just long enough to milk the moment without offending his new client.

Sam drove an ageing car that once again was of indeterminate origin. On getting in Mark was at once overwhelmed by the powerful scent of roses. Three big garlands of frangipani blossom were hanging from the rear view mirror. The scent of these was overpowering and the view ahead substantially impaired. He reached automatically for the seat belt but there wasn't one. Sam was tickled. He pointed out that in Samoa such things weren't really necessary and once they had set off Mark soon understood why as they creamed along at a noble nine miles an hour.

To begin with this was maddening, but it wasn't very long before he started to feel his residual tension dissolving away. The journey along the coast road was like a descent into a lost world. The vegetation surrounding them was dense and oppressive, a sea of dark green punctuated by huge and brilliant flowers. The sea itself was a sheet of blue glass away to the left. The frangipani scent began to dissipate somewhat now that they were moving – or just about moving – and it now mingled deliciously with the damp, musty exhalations of the rainforest.

As motorists they were in the minority of road users, swinging lazily and continuously to avoid dogs and chickens. Small black pigs were everywhere, scuffing about. Occasionally a crab the size of a tea tray would saunter unconcernedly across the road like a sacred cow and was duly afforded the same respect. The equality was humbling and Mark felt a quick pang of shame for his own headlong, hedgehog-splatting society.

Humans also occupied the road, wandering phlegmatically along with baskets of coconuts or bunches of bananas swinging from yolks across their shoulders, or just wandering along. Everyone was wrapped in colourful fabrics – the ubiquitous sarong was, he learned, known locally as a 'lavalava' – and many of the men were adorned extensively with elaborate and traditional-looking tattoos. Everyone, men and women alike, moved with a noticeable grace and fluidity that was immediately affecting, not to say seductive. These were bodies, he thought, that had never been tense. These were people who knew nothing of stress.

They passed through villages – clusters of huts in clearings in the rainforest. Sam explained that these huts were called 'farlays'. Each consisted of a ring of pillars cut from palm trunks supporting a thatched dome roof. None had any walls, though they did have woven screens that they could let down against the rain. Domestic security did not appear to be a concern for these people. Mark felt a long way from home. Sam told him that Samoan houses had been built this way for thousands of years. Partly it was for practical reasons, given the climate, but more particularly he said it was the 'Fa'a Samoa' – the 'Way of the Ancestors'. "Your house must be open" he said "so people can come." Mark felt a very long way from home.

He was just framing a line of questions for Sam when his informative driver got in first and asked him was he from Australia, New Zealand or America? When Mark replied that he was actually from England Sam gasped and said, in hushed tones: "Oh that is very, very far from my country." His face screwed up as he struggled with the concept of someone travelling such a distance, then he gave up and decided that his passenger must in fact be American, or possibly Australian. Mark was very affected by this and jealous of the man's innocence. He could comprehend as far as the Pacific rim, anywhere beyond that and it might as well have been Mars. As a child Mark had been enthralled with the notion of places that were immensely distant. That sense of wonderment had weakened with the encroaching prosaic realities of adulthood and for years he had been nostalgic for those feelings. Sam made him wish that he lived in a time when the world was larger and more mysterious. For him it clearly still was and for the first time Mark began to appreciate fully just how small and isolated this place really was.

He had expected Apia to feel both remote and exotic and his first impressions did not disappoint him. A sleepy south sea island port strung out around a sheltered bay, on one side a wharf where the copra boats came and went, on the other a vegetable market. Between, the harbour front was lined with what he thought of as nineteenth century colonial style buildings. White-washed, wooden, two storey villas with rusty iron roofs and verandahs running all round. Mostly given over to shops and offices, they graced the waterfront with a faded tropical splendour. A few modern buildings sat incongruously amongst them, while in the streets behind a haphazard collection of flimsier structures rotted quietly away in the steamy air.

The people moved serenely about in the wide streets, wrapped in their colourful lavalavas and seeming mostly to glide rather than walk. A few lorries chugged around, brightly painted in cheerful defiance of the final stages of decay. One rattled past him, on its back a wooden cage full of people laughing and chattering. He realised, after a moment, that it was a local bus and its noisy progress was punctuation in the silence, a foil to the deep tranquillity of the place.

Mark thought of one of his favourite passages from Conrad, in An Outcast of the Islands where there is a character who '... *drifted mysteriously in ... from the wastes of the Pacific, and, after knocking about for a time in the eddies of town life, had drifted out enigmatically into the sunny solitudes of the Indian Ocean.*' Well Apia felt like just that sort of place. The little bars along the waterfront looked as thought they might be full of Conrad's drifters – shady traders and opportunists with mysterious pasts – he half expected to be hustled at any moment by Humphrey Bogart.

He stayed at Aggie Grey's Hotel. He had read about Aggie – one of the South Pacific's legendary characters – who sadly had died only a year or so earlier. Originally she had run a small bar, which soon became a guest house, and business flourished during the Second World War when the place became a sanctuary for American servicemen. Aggie was widely tipped as having been the model for 'Bloody Mary' in Michener's *Tales from the South Pacific*. The hotel was now a fine place – rooms and fales clustered around a large pool and bar area. Everywhere there were tropical flowers and palms growing and guests helped themselves to bananas straight from the trees. In the evening they were summoned to dinner by the sound of the waiters drumming on a hollow log and they ate Polynesian cuisine in the open air, engulfed by the all-pervading rose-like scent of frangipani blossom.

Seven

Uncle Bill's contact in Samoa was, by local standards, a wealthy man. Originally from Fiji, he ran a profitable business exporting assorted coconut products from his own large plantation. Bill had written to him about his nephew's planned visit and had given Mark his telephone number. After settling into his room at the hotel Mark decided it might be a good first move to call him up: "Mr Olosega? It's Mark Fletcher - Bill Fletcher's nephew from England. I..."

"Mark, yes yes, how wonderful, you actually made it all this way then? And perfect timing my boy - I'm just off to the rugby. Where are you ... Aggies? I'll pick you up in five minutes, wait by the front door." With that he hung up and Mark was left sitting on his bed, more than a little perplexed. But he dutifully went and stood outside the front of the hotel and was surprised minutes later to see a sleek, silver Mercedes swoop gracefully to a halt at his feet. The door opened and out jumped Mafalu Olosega. Dressed in a white shirt, open sandals and a dazzling polychromatic sarong, he didn't look much like a tycoon, but as the country's largest exporter of coconut products, in Samoan terms he certainly was. Mild-mannered and charming, he insisted straight away on being called 'Mafu' and drove at a reckless fifteen miles an hour towards the edge of town.

Apia Park is a rugby pitch with a simple grandstand on one side and a hill blanketed with coconut palms on the other. Mafu's status afforded them entry to the VIP section of the stand and there, within hours of arriving in Western Samoa Mark found himself sitting directly behind the Prime Minister, the First Lady, the New Zealand Ambassador and the entire Samoan Cabinet. While Mafu exchanged pleasantries with his brother-in-law - the Minister for Overseas Trade - Mark sat and stared at the Prime Minister. Not just because he was the Prime Minister - although this fact, or rather that of his sudden proximity, was strange enough - but because he had never before seen such a wide, round man. The body seemed almost perfectly spherical and was of an immense girth. Mark was genuinely worried that if the man leaned too far forward he would, in all probability roll off his perch and bounce down the stand like a great beachball, crushing unfortunate spectators as he went.

His attention was at last wrested from the great expanse of flesh by the arrival of the players. The reason for all these dignitaries being assembled was that they were to observe the finals of the Pacific Cup. To open the show the national teams of Tonga and the Cook Islands battled for third place. The crowd of two thousand or so followed the play minutely - every positive move drawing roars of approval and every mistake, however small, being celebrated with gales of laughter and derisive whistling. Tonga won, but the result itself did not appear to be of much interest to anyone and no sooner had the players left the pitch than it was reclaimed, to the deafening approval of the crowd, by the home team. Western Samoa were to contest the cup itself with a formidable team of Maoris from New Zealand. The crowd seemed transported onto some preternatural plane of excitement - every good move by the Samoans brought carols of ecstasy and with every run by them of more than a few yards rhapsodic music poured from tinny tannoy speakers.

The pleasure felt by the crowd was intense and hopelessly infectious and Mark was amazed when a fight broke out down at the front of the stand. Awareness of the small commotion spread like wildfire and the entire crowd stood and craned their necks to see. But with impeccable timing Western Samoa chose this very moment to score their one and only try of the match and the event passed completely unnoticed. The players stopped in their tracks and stared bewilderedly at the silent stand. The crowd, realising that the players were not moving, stared back equally bewildered. For an awful moment it seemed as though the entire world had come to a halt and nobody quite knew why. Nobody that is but the tannoy operator who obviously wasn't able to see the fight from where he sat. The solemn music that wafted over the stand was so dreary that Mark knew it must be the National Anthem. When they heard it the crowd at last understood what had happened and, remaining on their feet, joined in with the words in an atmosphere of great awe. The music was noble and plodding and rose through a gradual crescendo to a passionate climax where two thousand souls tossed back their heads and sang "We are Samoa - people of the sun." At that very moment the sky cracked open and Apia Park was buried under a fantastic downpour. The players disappeared from view in an instant; one end of the stand was not visible from the other. But then, just as had happened the day before in Pago Pago, the Great Tap was turned off. In the flick of a switch the torrent of water was turned into one of ultra-violet and the steam rose audibly around them.

The Maoris played slick, if brutal rugby and won convincingly. No-one seemed to mind much though. 'How could you possibly mind' thought Mark 'after having such a good time?' As they left the ground Mafu sprung a further surprise by announcing that they were both invited to the post-match reception which was to be held almost immediately in a harbour-front restaurant. Mark insisted on dropping by the hotel to change, even though Mafu was confident that a steaming tee-shirt and shorts were entirely appropriate for the occasion. And he was right - it turned out to be a very informal gathering, despite many speeches from the four captains, various officials and, most notably, from the Prime Minister himself; though since they all spoke either in

Samoan or some other Polynesian language Mark had no idea what was said.

The beer, a delicious local brew called Vailima, was free and free-flowing, and while he sat chatting to Mafu, Mark cheerfully swallowed a very great deal of it. However, he had had nothing to eat all day and the physical stability of his surroundings soon became less than reliable. The insecurity he always felt in these circumstances was horribly heightened by the proximity of the Prime Minister, who held court at the very next table. The thought of embarrassing himself in front of Mafu was not something he relished, but to be drunk in front of the Prime Minister - that was too awful to contemplate and he struggled to get a grip.

He was painfully hungry by this time and urgently in need of solids, but at length, and to his enormous relief, a waitress brought a tray of food to the table. However this turned out to consist of nothing except raw fish. "Mmm ... sashimi" said Mafu, plunging a large piece into a thin and innocuous looking dip and devouring it with relish. Thus encouraged, Mark followed suite, but no amount of chicken vindaloo could ever have prepared him. If he had dropped a burning coal into his mouth he would not have been in more distress. It was several minutes before he could speak, during which time he sweated what seemed like his entire body weight in fluid and consumed countless cold bottles. But even as he did so, the world around him deteriorated into a manic, swirling blur. The only thing he could clearly remember later was a feeling of great anxiety about what he should say. All he could assume from this was that he had indeed been introduced to the Prime Minister, though to his everlasting shame he had no clear recollection of the event.

That night he dreamed of childhood Sunday lunches as though recalling a past life - cool rain outside and the eternally comforting smells of roast beef and Yorkshire pudding wafting warmly from the kitchen. Sunday morning in Samoa was bright blue and blisteringly hot, though the air was every bit as soggy as usual. Mark had been invited to Sunday lunch with Mafalu's family. He was pleased about this, though not so much for the insights into Polynesian culture it offered, but chiefly because he was still absolutely starving. His anticipation was only slightly tempered by nagging anxieties - would there be cultural mores he was ignorant of? Would he have to eat revolting things? But overall he was looking forward to it and felt quite excited as he sat in the bar waiting for Mafu to collect him.

The Olosega's home turned out to be a sprawling bungalow situated in what was clearly the more affluent end of town. The regulation corrugated iron roof sat atop glassless windows where rolled woven screens hung, poised to defend against the rain. Mark and Mafu sat in the spacious lounge like gentlemen in some colonial club while various members of the family filed in to be introduced and kept them supplied with ice cold jugs of lime cordial, freshly squeezed from the garden and extremely delicious.

In due course they were summoned to eat and found a large table groaning under an enormous quantity of food, far more it seemed than those seated around (Mafu, Mark, Mafu's wife, three sons and eldest daughter) could possibly manage. But Mafu's family was so large they could not all eat at the same time, so a second sitting later consisted of two more daughters, three daughters-in-law and several older grandchildren. Last in the pecking order, a great gaggle of younger grandchildren finally had their patience rewarded.

All the food had been prepared in the same way - wrapped in foil and baked - but the family were very concerned that Mark should not witness the realities of this process as they were certain his western sensibilities were not ready for their traditional ways and it would, to say the least, take the edge off his appetite. A fire had been laid in a pit in the back garden. Onto this stones had been placed which were then heated up to a great temperature. A quantity of water was thrown over and then the food - wrapped in foil parcels - before the whole thing was quickly sealed over with turf. After several hours it was all dug up and served. There was chicken, pork, beef steak, shark fillets and chicken curry. A bowl of fish roe, dark green and salty, was a great delicacy as it was only available for two months of the year. Huge prawns, not much smaller than lobsters; glutinous balls of sticky rice and small baked bananas which were used for mopping up juices. All of this was quite delicious, a sumptuous meal that they ate with their fingers and washed down with copious drafts of lime juice. But there was also taro, a root vegetable that is a staple food throughout Polynesia, though Mark could not imagine why since eating it was rather like he imagined it would be if his mouth were full of drying glue. The leaves were also eaten, folded into little parcels and filled with coconut cream then steamed. This was called Palusami and was offered to him as another traditional staple food, but he found it's stale, acrid flavour completely revolting and couldn't even force himself to eat more than one mouthful. He worried that they would be offended when he left what was on his plate but they didn't seem to mind. Mafu then pushed a large bowl of murky water in front of him and urged him to try it. Cautiously he probed the liquid with a knife. Something gelatinous floated to the surface. Seeing Mark's bewildered expression Mafu informed him that it was an octopus, though Mark was more inclined to think that a giant had blown his nose into the pot. He wasn't sure if the creature was raw or had been boiled into oblivion and he refused it politely, uncertain as to whether he was committing a cultural faux-pas but very certain it was worth the risk. In any event he was very full by this time and couldn't have eaten much more even if he had wanted to.

The stillness and immense heat of the afternoon were conspiring together with the effects of the enormous meal to make him decidedly sleepy and as Mafalu drove him slowly back to the hotel he dozed off completely. As they rolled to a halt outside Aggie's he came suddenly round and apologised profusely but Mafu laughed and bade him a cheerful farewell, promising he would ring in a day or two to arrange to have dinner.

*

Apia's fruit and vegetable market was a squelchy and aromatic place. People arrived from the countryside with produce to sell and simply lived in the market until it had all gone, sitting all day then sleeping in the same spot and living, he presumed, off their own merchandise. He had visions of some poor farmer with no sales technique dragging a great load of bananas twenty miles to market , eating them all himself and returning home penniless. Mark's experience of market places in Third World countries was limited, but this, although certainly a colourful enough place, seemed oddly calm. Many of the vendors were elderly and had long ago lost the generally exquisite bodies of their sons and daughters. For the most part they were slumped askew on rusting iron chairs; chatting, dozing and fanning themselves lazily in the steam-heat.

Mark felt slightly conspicuous as the only Westerner around; the more so because his clothes and expensive-looking camera clearly marked him out as a tourist. Relative to all these people he was a wealthy man. He had read in his guide book that the United Nations described Western Samoa as a 'least developed country' - squarely part of the Third World. Throughout the time he had been planning this trip he had expected to come here and find an impoverished people looking out at the western world with envy. What he found instead was a happy, hospitable people with no obvious interest in, or need for, other people's money. He had managed to find a couple of shops in Apia selling tee shirts and wooden carvings but otherwise there were few concessions to tourism.

Everything they needed to sustain themselves seemed to grow abundantly all around them, without them even having to make any effort to cultivate: it was simply a matter of harvesting the coconuts, bananas, pineapples, taro and seafood. Whatever Samoans saw the purpose of life as being, it certainly wasn't the pursuance of mamon - they seemed quite content just to be.

If in the market he had been besieged by people waving artefacts in his face he might have felt more comfortable as a tourist, more justified in his role. As it was, standing there with his Minolta around his neck and nobody taking the slightest notice of him, he began to feel rather uncomfortable. Even taking a few photographs felt morally suspect. He realised that he had gone to the market in much the same spirit as he might have visited a zoo - primarily to take pictures that he could show around his family and friends back home who would pore over them and use words like 'fascinating' and 'ethnic'.

He retreated to the tourist sanctuary of Aggie's hotel and settled into the bar with a bottle of Vailima. Unusually for him he found himself chatting to some fellow guests - Robert and Susan were from Hobart and had arrived the day before on the once-a-week plane from Sydney with the intention of spending their honeymoon in paradise. It turned out that Susan had also been to the market that morning, but instead of standing around like a twit she had sat with a group of women and learned the traditional method of weaving baskets from pandanus leaves. Despite the language barrier she had learned much about their lifestyle and they hers. Another little confirmation. Mark had always quietly suspected that other people were, in some unfathomable way, connected to each other, to the world, while he always stood apart, watching, as though from behind a glass.

The following day he joined Robert and Susan, a handful of other guests from the hotel and a local guide - Sam (not his taxi driver) - for an expedition to another island. They travelled initially in a small minibus. In front of Mark sat a middle-aged couple from Sydney, she Australian, he an expatriate German who spoke with a curious mix of violent gutturals and Aussie strine. In front of them sat a German couple with whom the expat quickly struck up a friendship, clearly relishing the chance to converse in his old mother tongue. His wife on the other hand understood not a word and took a dim view of this enforced social exclusion. Her interjections became less and less polite as things went on, but were nevertheless largely ignored. Expat was determined to enjoy himself and stuck doggedly to his guns, his eyes betraying a smouldering impatience with his wife.

As the tension rose between them so did the interest of the other passengers; only the Germans themselves appearing to be unaware of what was happening. Mark found himself torn between the prehistoric jungle landscape they were passing through and the drama that was unfolding in the next seat. Both demanded his full attention. By the time they came to a halt at the north-west tip of the island Expat was still basking in linguistic nostalgia and his wife by now was keeping the pressure on with a terrible silence.

At this part of 'Upolu the coral reef that surrounds the island arcs a few miles out to sea and encloses the tiny, low, palm covered island of Manono - Michener's 'Bali-Hai'. To travel the two miles or so across the lagoon Sam invited them all to climb aboard a small, elegantly shaped wooden boat that perched enticingly on the beach. Mark observed, with a whiff of familiarity, that it was extremely old and shabby but brightly painted. It also sported a two-stroke engine and a flimsy canvas canopy. Expat's face registered pure horror.

A little squall was playing around some distance away to the north, but no-one had paid much attention as it looked to be a good few miles away. However, just as they reached about half way across it drew ominously closer, then all of a sudden bore savagely down upon them, drilling a ferocious path between the islands. The sea boiled around them, the rain was suffocating, the little boat surfed and swooped like a roller-coaster. Some people screamed, most clung grimly to their seats and all of them struggled to protect their cameras. Mark comforted himself with the hopeful thought that local boatmen must surely know what they are doing - Sam's friend on the tiller certainly looked nonchalant enough, managing to ride his bucking bronco with serene implacability despite having to endure the most thorough soaking.

But the squall passed as suddenly as it had come, leaving them bobbing about on a choppy sea, and it was with general relief that they came into smooth water in the lee of the island and slid quietly onto a lovely white sand beach. They took of their shoes, hitched up their skirts and hopped over the side knee deep into a warm bath. Mark's guide book had told him the sea temperature in the lagoons averaged eighty-three Fahrenheit, but as he had not yet been for a swim he hadn't fully appreciated what this meant; the shock of the warm water now was glorious and rather strange.

The little party collected themselves on the beach, and once the stage was set and the audience in position Expat finally gave vent to his anger. He rounded on the hapless Sam with a tirade of abuse, the central thrust of which was that 'you people' simply couldn't treat tourists this way. What was the matter with him? Expat asked, hands and shoulders arcing heavenwards. Couldn't he at least have found a proper boat for them? How dare he put all their lives at risk in such a heap of shit after they had paid him good money! Hadn't they ever heard of jetties in this country? And what about life jackets? If he didn't look after his clients' safety and comfort then he would go out of business and serve him damn well right! Poor old Sam just stared at him in blank bewilderment. The Germans nodded in silent, sombre agreement. His wife appeared to have forgotten all about her own anger and stood beside him now, flushed with pride and looking for all the world like Nancy Reagan.

The rest of the group meanwhile, not being particularly excited by Expat's display, were milling about on the beach, taking in the scenery and generally having rather a good time of it. For Mark, just to be in such a place at all was exciting beyond words and all the more exhilarating for the feeling that he had reached well beyond the range of currently developed tourism. They wandered in a straggling file along the beach, their wet clothes drying visibly in the fierce sunshine, then Sam led them off into the rainforest along a rough track. The vegetation was smothering and the hot air became steamier. It felt as if they were the first humans to ever set foot in the place. After a while they came to a small village of primitive huts that looked as though they had mushroomed out of the leaf-mould a thousand years before. Excited children ran up to them, naked and wide-eyed. One little boy, not more than four or five years old, carried a beautiful conch shell, bigger than his own head, which he proudly showed off. Nancy Reagan made strenuous efforts to buy it from him and when at last he understood what she wanted he clutched it to his chest and ran away, crying. The grown-ups were more timid and watched from the safety of their fales, covering their eyes and giggling whenever a camera was pointed at them.

Coming again to the water they passed through a second village where little dug-out canoes reclined gracefully at the edge of the lagoon after the morning's fishing. At length they arrived at a secluded and beautiful beach. Expat came up beside Mark, stretched his arm at the view and said: "Ach ... der rrrreal Polynesia." Mark nodded slowly and tried hard not to smile. He translated this confident declaration as 'Ah ... at long last something that actually looks like what Polynesia is supposed to look like.' He wasn't angry with Expat; tourists are the real victims of tourism, he thought.

There was no denying it was a classically Polynesian scene and the poor man may well have seen something similar in a book or a film, but he wouldn't, Mark knew, have recognised 'der rrrreal Polynesia' if it crept up behind him and stuck a coconut up his arse.

The following day Mark, Robert and Susan had Sam to themselves and the four of them escaped into the hills in a small minibus. Travelling first along the coast road towards the eastern end of 'Upolu, they soon turned inland and began to climb through the rainforest along roads of soft earth that doubled as rivers every time it rained - which at this time of year was several times a day. The resulting surface guaranteed an extremely uncomfortable ride and the resilience of the little bus's suspension was amazing. But Sam had had the foresight to bring along several large cool boxes, each full of nicely chilled beer and as the journey went on the three, being thus well watered, became increasingly philosophical about the rigours of jungle travel.

As they ascended they were met with some startlingly dramatic vistas; the craggy, forest-covered volcanic landscape put Mark in mind of Conan Doyle's 'Lost World.' They passed through primitive villages that were muddy and indolent and it was a big surprise, when they were halted in one village by a huge and noisy gaggle of school children, to find them wearing uniform bright red sarongs and sparkling white shirts. The children swarmed around them, squeaky-clean and doe-eyed, exploding with a mass joy verging on hysteria every time a shutter clicked. Their teacher was the worst; he begged Mark to take his photograph and when his pleas were rewarded he bounced up and down in a sort of crazed paroxysm.

Sam explained that parents in Samoa took enormous pride in things like school uniforms but that they often had to make sacrifices in order to provide them. In fact they had to pay for everything at school - books, pens - the government provided very little in the way of equipment. His explanation of this was that by far the greater part of the national product went on building churches and Mark could easily believe him judging by the number of such buildings he had seen. Every village, no matter how small, had it's own little centre of worship. Many of them were not even small but four-square, castellated structures - impressive and quintessentially tropical - their white-washed walls standing out against the dark green of the forest as stark monuments to the success of missionary zeal.

After bumping their way down the other side of 'Upolu's craggy spine for more than an hour they eventually arrived at a village called Lalomanu - a lovely, lilting name, Mark thought, for a place that boasted the most beautiful beach he had ever seen. A gently shelving crescent of pure white powdery sand, fringed by huge palm trees that craned languid necks towards the water, the whole cradling a tranquil, translucent and absurdly blue sea. A couple of small boys from the village were down by the water's edge fiddling with a fishing basket, otherwise there wasn't a soul to be seen. Early that morning Sam had been to the market and from a cool box he produced a small but whole and perfectly fresh tuna fish which he proceeded to barbecue while the others languished in the warm, shallow water drinking beer.

Though small for a tuna, the fish was large and fat and it seemed there would be far too much for the four of them to eat. But before long another minibus arrived with eight or nine others from the hotel - Expat and Nancy among them. Mark felt a ripple of dismay, but it passed over him - he simply couldn't be bothered to feel irritable in such privileged and gorgeous surroundings. The tuna was delicious and quite unlike anything that comes in a tin. But the real treat came after - Sam handed him a slice of pineapple the size of a large dinner plate. The scale of the thing was surprise enough, but eating it proved to be a revelation. Sweeter, juicier and more succulent than any fruit he had ever eaten before, this was pleasure in it's purest form. His teeth sank satisfyingly through intensely aromatic flesh. The juice - nectar he would call it - ran down his chin and onto his stomach. And this was perhaps the most gratifying part - a sudden flashback to infancy when food was such an all-encompassing satisfaction and being in a mess didn't matter a bit. *'Do I dare to eat a peach?'* ... he thought of his favourite poem...

'I shall wear white flannel trousers and walk upon the beach. I have heard the mermaids singing each to each.'

Eight

Early one morning, a couple of days later, Mark found himself standing, luggage in hand, on a set of scales at the edge of a field while an elderly man carefully measured his weight. The man was very smartly dressed in a blue formal lavalava (unpatterned, wrapped like a kilt and belted) and a crisp, clean white shirt. His assistant was a rangy youth with a frizzy shock of hair, an oily tee-shirt and an informal lavalava (bright, floral and held up by a couple of twists at the front). A taxi pulled up and the three were joined by an elderly couple who, in turn, were duly weighed. Mark leaned across and read their luggage labels - they were New Zealanders, from Wanganui, and engaging them in conversation proved a fruitless task. They scarcely spoke a word to each other, let alone to anyone else and it flashed in his mind that they might be the Wanganui Debating Society having a rest.

They were in up the hills behind Apia, a few miles from town at a tiny airstrip called Fagali'i. The taxi driver had been mystified until Mark produced a map. He had forgotten that all 'g's in Polynesia are pronounced 'ng' and this apparently minor slip had left the man with not the remotest idea where he wanted to go.

Not far from the scales stood a petrol pump and a garden shed. The shed turned out to be the terminal building and the three were invited to make themselves comfortable inside while they waited for their flight. It was only eight in the morning but the heat was already considerable and there wasn't a cloud to be seen in the brilliantly blue sky. For a while nothing disturbed the silence, then a faint buzzing could just be heard; distant, but it grew steadily louder until at last a dinky little aeroplane swooped over the field and came bumping to a halt beside the petrol pump. It was so small that he wondered at first if it might be somebody's radio-controlled toy, but then a robust looking Australian pilot sprang athletically through the door dispensing cheerful "G'day's". An equally robust looking Australian woman with a baby strapped to her chest appeared from nowhere and offered him a cup of tea from a thermos before vanishing as mysteriously as she had come. The oily boy unravelled a length of hose pipe from the pump, climbed up on a stool and stuck it in the wing.

When he was done they all climbed aboard. Mark sat directly behind the pilot and found he had a splendid view of all the controls and out through the cockpit windscreen. The pilot tossed a safety instructions card into his lap and cheerfully added that it didn't take much working out with a door at the end of each arm. He opened the throttles and the noise from the engines was deafening as they bounced along the field. But then Polynesian Airlines flight PH330 Domestic Service lifted above the grass, dangled uncertainly for a moment, then rose smoothly and steeply into the bright, clear air.

As the little plane levelled out at about two thousand feet he had a breath-taking view of the coral reefs that surround 'Upolu. Great white swirling banks divided the deep blue of the sea from the sparkling aquamarine of the lagoons. He gazed and gazed, knowing full well that this was a scene he would remember for the rest of his life and wanting to drink every drop of it in. It was exhilaration, pure and complete.

They were flying to the island of Savai'i - much the largest in Samoa - a fat, tear-drop shape about forty miles long and separated from 'Upolu by a thirteen mile channel. The whole island slopes gradually and almost uniformly up to a central spine of volcanoes, some of which are still active. Mount Silisili, at around six thousand feet being the highest point in all of Samoa. When Mark had sat down all those months before and looked at his map, he had considered the tiny village of Asau, nestled in a cove near the north-west tip of Savai'i, and pictured it as a possible setting for Thomas's escape from the *Pandora*, of his subsequent life and indeed of his meeting with William. When he enquired at the Polynesian Airlines office in Apia about the possibilities of going over to Savai'i he was bowled over to discover not only that Asau possessed one of only two airstrips on the island, but that a plane went there every day and he would be able to stay in a little hotel right on the beach - the very beach where Thomas and William could have met.

They skirted around the north coast of the island, descended, swung sharply round above a glittering blue lagoon and perched daintily on a tiny airstrip that must, at one time, have been part of the coral reef. They came to a halt beside yet another garden shed, and though it was even smaller than the one at Fagali'i, a faded Air New Zealand poster pinned to the wall indicated that this was indeed the terminal building.

A small minibus picked them up and drove them along a bumpy dirt road through the rainforest, which was peppered with small boulders of black volcanic rock. The village itself was a straggling mixture of old wooden buildings and traditional thatched huts. After passing through it they turned off the road and descended along a rough track through dense undergrowth, at length arriving at another, equally run-down collection of aged wooden buildings - all faded yellow-brown paint and rusty-red corrugated iron roofs. This was the Mana-Kai Hotel. It nestled among palm trees and peeped out at it's own exquisite little bay. Thomas and William's bay. A talcum powder beach beside a lagoon of the bluest blue that anyone could imagine, framed by gently swaying coconut palms and quite deserted. It was a secret and wonderful place.

Things seemed to happen in slow motion. The only sound was the distant rustle of breakers out on the reef. Ever since his arrival in Pago Pago Mark had felt himself to be floating around in some sort of dream world, but here he felt certain he was entering an inner sanctum - a holy place - enchanted, silent, melancholic and inexpressibly tranquil.

His roomboy was called Sam. He was beginning to take it for granted that all Samoan men were called Sam. He watched him glide away down the path with his bags but didn't follow; instead he was seduced into the lounge bar, a comfortably shabby room with a huge curving verandah that gave out onto the beach. Slow ceiling fans churned the steamy air; Lauren Bacall draped herself sultrily across the bar and blew languid smoke rings at Edward G Robinson.

Mark slouched on a stool and began to soak up the atmosphere - torpid but intense. After a while he turned slightly and saw a young native man walking across the room. He was wearing a bright lavalava and a tee-shirt. The power of the sinews beneath his garments was almost tangible as he walked and the naturalness and grace of his movements was absolute. His face was beautiful, placid and radiant. As he came nearer he looked straight at Mark, his eyes shone and the beginings of a smile played on his lips. He turned his head as he walked and kept his eyes fixed on Mark almost until he was out of the room.

As he watched him go Mark was aware of a slight frisson , but whether it was of panic or excitement he wasn't quite sure. Something about that smile - that look - had unsettled him slightly and he sensed that he knew why, but the awareness wasn't quite at the surface yet.

He drank a couple of beers and enjoyed a sensuous slice of fresh pineapple then went and found his room, had a shower and sat on his balcony sipping tea, entirely naked and feeling at that moment that he was unquestionably the luckiest man on earth. He had no real idea how many hours he sat there in the silence, gazing at the blue water. Over the years, on his various travels, he had seen plenty of stunning blues; but he had never seen blue like this. He wouldn't have believed that such a blue could exist if he hadn't been looking at it now with his very own eyes; wouldn't have believed that blue could ever be quite this blue. It wasn't one of those ocean blues that are almost purple, beautiful but common in hot countries, it was just blue - just blue - the rarest, deepest, clearest, simplest, most intense, most profound - blue. And he stared at it - just stared - and stared - and stared - for hours. He didn't even mind - now that the knowledge had surfaced - that the young man's smile had been one of recognition.

His decision to go snorkelling wasn't really a conscious one - in fact it wasn't really a decision at all - he simply reached a point where he felt so much a part of this great blue that to go and be in the middle of it seemed as natural as taking his next breath. The water was warm - extremely warm - warmer even than a swimming pool. He put his mask on, entered fully and found himself hanging suspended, rocking gently to and fro, any tension that was left in him (and there wasn't much) running out through his arms and legs as they trailed in the lovely liquid. How many times as a child had he dreamed of vaulting through his bedroom window and swooping serenely around the garden? The desire to fly had never really left him, and here he was, soaring twenty feet above smooth white sand in what appeared to be an immense blue crystal. He could see at least a hundred metres in every direction with absolute clarity. Shafts of sunlight arrowed down, dappling the bottom and throwing off showers of sparkling flashes as a million tiny iridescent fish swam through them. At intervals there were islands of coral, small clumps or great banks with an endless array of colours and shapes - branching stag-horns white and black, rose-pink fans ten feet across. In places it grew in thick towers that reached almost to the surface and here, if he was careful, he could climb out and sit, surveying the quiet blue surface while warm tongues licked and lapped his legs, calling him back - calling him back.

Most of the coral was in full sunlight and the colours were astonishing. Each clump was surrounded by a profusion of life

- fish of every size, shape, colour and pattern he could have imagined, and many that he never would have. Bright blue starfish half a metre across lolled about on the coral, troupes of yellow sea-horses twitched imperiously, shoals of brilliantly shiny fish teemed and exploded in every direction as he plunged into them. It was a ravishing experience.

Some of the fish were inquisitive and confident, at times swimming right up to him. As he floated over one particular coral garden, feeling exactly like some ponderous aircraft, a few of the braver characters even administered warning pecks on his toes. He was keenly aware that this was not an aquarium but the real thing - the wild. There he was in the midst of a whole community of life forms, unendingly diverse and all perfectly at home in this alien world where his own physical resources held no currency. It was every bit as humbling as it was thrilling and only a fear of sunburn forced him to drag himself away. As he walked up onto the white powdery beach he felt himself emerging from a dream - a dream within a dream.

A little way down the beach a small structure was built out over the water on posts, by Mark's estimation a good few years ago. A narrow, flimsy walkway led out to what looked like yet another old garden shed, but this one had a verandah running around it. The clinker-board walls were painted in a fading dirty-orange and it's roof was of the ubiquitous corrugated iron. He wandered over, and judging the walkway safe enough, took the thirty or so steps out to the shed. Peering through glassless windows he saw the remains of what had once been a bar. He could only guess at how long ago it had fallen into disuse and he lamented it greatly, for what more perfect location could there be? But it lay silent, stools broken and tumbled about, the wooden bar curling up with damp and the musty smell strong, even from outside. He sat down on the verandah, dangling his legs over the edge and listened to the slight slapping and sucking of the water against the posts while he stared, first at the white beach and deep green coconut palms, then out into the blue...

A small canoe was resting by the water's edge. A rough craft fashioned from a tree trunk, it was perhaps ten feet long and had a small outrigger. He had passed it as he set off for his swim earlier and been struck by how primitive it looked. His attention was now drawn back to it because a young Samoan, perhaps in his early twenties, was busying himself around it, fiddling with a fishing net and some baskets. He was very pre-occupied with his work and didn't seem to notice Mark staring at him. 'Now there' said Mark to himself 'is a body to be proud of.' His connoisseur's eye quickly took in the balanced pro-portions, the controlled strength, the easy - almost balletic movements. The man's shoulders were square-set and bulbous, his chest deep, his stomach ribbed. A colourful lavalava was wrapped around his tidy waist, at first masking his lower body; but soon he stepped into the water in order to launch his canoe and when he re-emerged Mark could see the wet fabric clinging to his powerful thighs. His smooth skin was the colour of pecan shells and he was crowned with a tight bush of curly black hair. It was the same young man who had stared at him earlier in the bar.

Apparently unaware of Mark's presence, much less of his attention, he sprang into the little boat and paddled out into the lagoon, stopping some fifty or so metres from the shore. At that distance Mark could clearly see the muscles of his back, firm and springy, stretching and contracting like fillets of rub-ber as he swung his shoulders and spun out his net. One side of the net sank rapidly and after only a minute or so he was hauling it in with quick, powerful movements. After picking over his catch he would again launch the net, a wonderful swing of his back and shoulders sending it spinning out over the water.

He kept to his work without respite for perhaps an hour or more and throughout this time Mark remained perfectly oblivious of anything else and did not take his eyes away. At length the fisherman hauled in his net for the last time, took up the paddle and headed back to the beach. Mark found it impossible to look away, even though as he drew closer it was clear he would pass within a few metres. But as he did so he finally noticed Mark, immediately waving and flashing a huge white grin. "Talofa" he shouted.

"Talofa" Mark called back. He had never heard the word before but assumed it must be a greeting. He returned the young man's smile and hoped that he didn't look as guilty or self-conscious as he certainly felt. He continued to watch as the young Samoan beached his canoe, laid the net out and carefully rolled it, then took a thick stick from the boat, hung a basket of fish from each end, swung it over his shoulder and walked off up the beach.

Mark returned to his room and lay on the bed. Straight away he imagined himself sprawled in the fisherman's canoe somewhere far out by the reef, his legs trailing over the sides in the warm water, his arms tangled helplessly in the net above his head while the young man's purposeful hands - now gentle, now cruel - coaxed him slowly to a spasming ecstasy. 'Oh William, William' he called aloud, 'now I understand what happened to you!'

In the six months since he had first written the story of William and Thomas he had revised it extensively and it had now grown almost to the length of a short novel. What it lacked, apart from a denouement, was any authentic sense of place. Up until now he had just been working from his imagination, although he had read as much as he could about Samoa and had found pictures in an old *National Geographic* in the library, he had had no real idea of what the place was actually like, or of what it would feel like to be here.

As things had evolved through his revisions Thomas had not disclosed his terrible secrets to William so readily, a long time had passed while the two got to know each other before he trusted the preacher enough to even consider it. Instead he had managed to allay his new friend's curiosity by telling, if not a white lie, then at least a partial truth about his departure from the *Pandora*. William had found himself to all intents and purposes adopted by Thomas and his family. In the early days he had made valiant attempts to talk to them about Jesus but it was all rather meaningless to them and they took scant notice of his stories. He had imagined that he would be based in Apia, assisting James Smith in establishing a mission there and finding himself instead stranded in such an isolated situation he was somewhat at a loss to know quite what to do. At the same time he was physically a fish out of water to a comprehensive degree and had a great deal to learn about his surroundings and about the Samoan way of life. All of this rather pre-occupied him and by the time several months had passed he found himself falling more and more easily into native ways and thinking less and less about The Lord.

But he was also becoming a troubled man for another reason. Thomas had a son - Jimmy - who was the same age as William and was, to the enormous concern of his parents, unmarried and not even courting. Jimmy was teaching William to fish from a canoe and so the two of them spent a great deal of time together away from the village, far out by the reef. Gradually, day by day, a certain sexual tension developed between them and William found himself having to confront his long-suppressed homosexuality. Being so far away from home and so cut off from anyone who might have helped or had any influence - including, it seemed, The Lord - he was somewhat helpless. His defences broke down easily, perhaps inevitably, and the two began a secret sexual relationship. At the same time however, Thomas grew to trust William and eventually, during a very protracted and painful late night conversation, he unburdened himself and told William the whole story of what happened with Harry Lamb, of the horror of Harry's subsequent flogging and of his total inability to come to terms with any of it since.

Thus an appalling triangle was established and as yet Mark had absolutely no idea how it was going to work out. Thomas had developed a great trust in the young preacher and now, having disclosed the most intimate information to him, had also made a great emotional investment. To then learn that William was secretly shagging his son would be devastating for him. Mark knew enough about Polynesian culture from his reading to suppose that while it may not have been unknown for teenagers to play about and experiment, an adult homosexual lifestyle would have been anathema to them and they would have had a tough time dealing with the fact of Jimmy's sexuality. Mark was no sociologist, but he understood that traditional Samoan life was based around the extended family and that certain things would be fundamental to them - tradition, continuity, group rather than individual identity, group survival and the duty to produce children. There would have been no room there for William and Jimmy. Perhaps, if they turned out to be really committed to each other and certain that this was what they wanted, they would go off and find some small uninhabited island where they could live off the land, fish the lagoon, never wear any clothes and lead an idyllic, if reclusive, existence. But then what of Thomas? Poor old Thomas - he didn't deserve to lose them. Perhaps he could go through a lengthy process of adjustment and ultimately come to terms with it all. Mark was well aware that by writing something like that he would inevitably be examining some of his own difficulties - a thing he studiously avoided but that he knew, deep-down, he couldn't put off for ever. The world of the Pandora was also starting to open up as he researched and wrote and here again he was aware that by imagining this detached and close-quartered world, by considering the ways and the tensions of this all-male society, he was starting, little by little, to acknowledge some of his own anxieties, his fantasies, his paranoia about the real-life men-only world that as yet he barely knew. He dug out his original sketch of Thomas's unburdoning and settled back to read it through.

"We sailed north, accompanied by the little schooner, and after some days arrived at an island called Aitutaki. Scarce an island at all really – just a crest of palm trees fringing a bright lagoon. A launch was dispatched, the party searched, but Christian was not there and we continued. We cast about in that group of islands, searching vigorously, but without success. The little schooner proved to be a remarkably seaworthy vessel though. Mr Oliver was put in charge of her and she outsailed the Pandora at every turn. Indeed she proved useful to us in our searches as being of shallow draft she could pass close inshore, clearing reefs much too dangerous for the Pandora to approach, and ferret about the lagoons looking for traces of the mutineers.

"As we left that group of islands and made passage over to these, which we knew then as the Navigator Islands, the weather grew foul again and the ship laboured in heavy seas. The crew became dispirited as the task of finding Fletcher Christian seemed ever more hopeless. But one night, as we were hove-to a mile or so off from this island and not very far from here, my whole life William was abruptly turned upside down.

"I had been skulking around on deck, not able to sleep, and was squatting by the poop deck gangway looking up at the stars. The moon was full and I could clearly see the breakers going over the reef about a mile off and the dark mass of the island – this island, Savai'i – beyond. All of a sudden Harry appeared in front of me. I was surprised to see him and he didn't seem to be his usual self. He was all agitated as if something was wrong. I asked him what was up but he told me to shush and then started talking right queer; saying he was sorry, over and over, and that he was desperate and couldn't bear it no more. 'I 'ave to 'ave a chew lad' he kept saying... 'I 'ave to .'ave a chew. You understand don't yer lad? It'll be alright, you'll see...I 'ave to 'ave a chew."

"I didn't know what he was talking about and I got right scared.

His breath was so short I fancied he was crying. But then without more ado he unbuttoned his breeches and his John Thomas was right there in front of my face, standing up to attention like a red faced soldier and reeking of piss. I wanted to get up and run of course, but I was so affeared I just froze to the spot. He kept saying it'd be alright, that he wasn't going to hurt me, that it wouldn't be so bad. Next thing I knew his great hands were round the back of my head, holding me in a grip, and he was pushing his thing into my mouth. I gagged and choked and my nose filled with the stench of it. I kept thinking I must have done something bad, something to really upset him and so he was punishing me. But why like this? I tried to get free but he had me in a vice of a grip. All I kept thinking was 'what have I done wrong? What ever did I do wrong?'

"I can't say how long it went on, but all at once his thing came out of my mouth, he let go of my head and fell backwards on the deck with a mighty crash. Lieutenant Parkin stood over us, fists clenched up and fairly bursting with rage. 'You foul creature!' he shouted – 'You foul, foul creature!' His voice shook with temper and his face was a good shade of purple. He bent over Harry and struck him again several times, each time bellowing at him – 'Foul...foul...foul!'

"By now several men of the watch had gathered about and I'm sure it was straight away obvious to all what had been taking place. Harry lay flat on his back with his breeches open and his angry John Thomas waving all about. I was squatting on all fours, spluttering and spewing onto the deck and sobbing without let up. I think Harry was out cold – Parkin was a brute of a man and had set about him with a purpose. Two of the men carried me below, splashed some water over my face and gave me a large tot of rum. It was fiery and burnt my throat but it took Harry's stench away and I was mighty grateful for that. 'Don't worry lad' said one of the men, 'that dirty bastard'll 'ave a red-checked shirt at the gangway in the morning and no mistake.' I had no idea what he meant. I went to my hammock and curled up tight but slept not a minute. I think there was never a lad more jangled up than I was that night William.

"In the morning the gratings were lifted and rigged at the gang-way. All the ship's company were mustered on deck and Captain Edwards called for Harry Lamb to step forward and remove his shirt. As soon as he had done so an order was given to seize him up. Two men led him to the gangway and lashed his wrists to the gratings, wide apart and far above his head. To my surprise the Captain called my name and for a terrible moment I thought I was to be seized up too, but he only wanted for me to stand where I should have a proper view. I knew by now that Harry was going to receive a flogging, but I had no idea what a spectacle of horror this would be. I'd heard men talk of navy beatings, of men's backs cut to ribbons and never healing over, but I never paid them much heed, thinking them to be just stories and set to scare a lad.

"Well the bosun stepped forward – I don't recall his name – and the Captain asked for two dozen. The bosun carried a small hessian bag and from this he pulled out the cat-o-nine-tails, uncoiling it and giving it a shake to free all the strands. With the first blow Harry let out a gasp – I think the breath was knocked clean out of him – and a great welt rose straight away, deep red and angry across his back. By the fourth or fifth his blood was running freely and his screams were terrible – more like an animal than a man. It was more than I could bear. I cast my eyes down at the deck and tried to block out the sound of his screaming, but the Captain saw me and shouted out that I should hold my head up and witness the punishment. He said that after what this man had done to me it was fit and proper that I should know what the navy did to beasts like him. He turned to the bosun and told him to 'lay on with a will.' After several lashes more I watched the man drag the cat through his fingers to free it of blood and bits of flesh and thereupon I fainted dead away. Coming back to myself with a jolt as they threw a pale of sea water over me, I saw them cut Harry's limp body from the gratings and carry him below. His back was a pulpy mess of red and purple with here and there a bit of bone showing.

"I can't give you any good idea of my state of mind William – if there are the words for it then I have never learned them. But presently Captain Edwards called for me and I was taken to the poop deck. I remember a feeling of great numbness and a burning desire to cry, but finding that I could not. He told me there was a break in the reef not far distant and that a landing party was to be dispatched ashore to search for signs of the mutineers. Moreover, that I was at liberty to go with them if I wished, as he considered this would help to take my mind away from the grimness of recent events.

"I took my seat in the launch and as we pulled away from the ship I was taken over with the most powerful desire to escape. With every pull of the oars I felt the Pandora and all the horrors she contained falling away behind me. I rocked back and forth, willing the boat onward. When we drove onto the beach I straight away felt the sand as a solid thing beneath the keel, secure, holding me, and I knew at that moment that I would not return to the ship, that I would never again put to sea.

"The men went about their business, separating into small parties and setting off on their searches. None of them took much notice of me. I dallied about at the top of the beach for a time, near to the line of the trees, and by and by wandered further into the forest. As soon as the men were at such a distance that I could no longer hear their voices I turned into the trees and ran. I ran William like I had never run, like the wind itself, and with every stride I seemed to grow lighter – every stride took me further from the horror. Behind me was a great weight and darkness but in front there was only light and I ran towards it.

"How long I was running I could not say, but it was a long time. I fell many times, my face was cut but I only noticed later, when I stopped. At length I fell to the ground and did not get up but lay exhausted. I had wanted to run forever but my body had reached its limits and so I lay there in the forest, panting for dear life.

"At length I thought of the men at arms and became concerned that they might find me. I concealed myself as best I could in some thick bushes and must have fallen asleep with sheer exhaustion as the next thing I knew it was dark and the air was somewhat cooler. I was quickly asleep again but was woken by voices. It was now daylight again and I could clearly hear English voices and some beating of the bushes. I crouched low in my little hideaway; I dared not run as they seemed so close I thought they would certainly see or hear me. But though I hear them I saw no-one and after a time the voices grew more distant as the men gave up their search and moved back down the hill.

"I remained in my hide-out in the bushes for many hours, not thinking of hunger or thirst, only affeared that the men at arms would appear and take me back to the ship. Through a gap in the trees I was able to see a small patch of blue ocean and more an more I found I was unable to take my eyes from it. I stared fixedly at the little patch of sea without understanding what my fascination was about. But after some time I saw the ship sail slowly across and out of my view. A cold panic ran through me as I realised what I had done. I knew that the ship had sailed and would not call here again; that I was stuck here and would not see England or my mother again. I screamed aloud and wept for the fool I was and took serious fright at the gravity of my situation. I wept and screamed and yelled —I screamed until my throat was sore.

"Presently I found myself surrounded by a group of native people. I presumed they had been alerted by my racket. I also presumed that they intended to cook and eat me and I should say that this prospect did not much trouble me at that moment. But they were kindly and took me to their village where they fed and cared for me. The rest of my tale I fancy I do not need to tell. So here you find me William, now that forty-four years have passed, and whatever must you think of me now?"

William regarded him with a mixture of compassion and admiration. "Well in faith Thomas it is a remarkable story, that is for certain, and one of which you should in no way be ashamed. You were a lad Thomas, you ran impulsively from a great horror as anyone would. In consequence you stranded yourself here, and although you have missed your mother it seems you nevertheless have enjoyed a good life. You surely cannot believe that you were in any way responsible for those terrible events Thomas, not for any of it."

"William, we must all be responsible for our actions and our circumstances."

"But you were a boy Thomas, a young slip of a lad and a grown man took advantage of you. A foul deed for sure, but one for which you could hold no culpability, none whatever. There was nothing you could have done. Thomas – please tell me you understand this – please tell me you have not lived all these years burdened with the guilt of this."

Thomas stared fixedly at the ground in front of him. Beads formed in the corners of his eyes and when at last he spoke his voice was tremulous and thin. "I have a wife and children, that is a fact, but I confess to you William – from that day to this I have always felt less than a man."

"No Thomas you are wrong. As God is my witness I say you are wrong about this and I pray with all my strength that you only needed to hear someone say so." The older man's face was now streaked with tears. William reached over and took his hand and the two of them sat in silence.

*

He thought he would have a shower, but when he turned on the tap all that emerged was a dribble of some substance rather like gravy, followed by nothing at all. So instead he made his way over to the bar like some amphibious sea creature, richly encrusted with salt and smelling strongly of sea water which he hoped a lavish coating of coconut oil would help to disguise.

His only companions on the verandah were a middle-aged couple from New York. He knew this because their distinctive drawl was so acute it seemed their cheeks must be stapled together. The man, for reasons best known to himself, wore a plastic mackintosh. Although late afternoon the temperature was still well into the nineties and there wasn't a cloud to be seen. He was bare-legged and completed his outfit with smart dark shoes and socks. The most intriguing thing about him though was the manner in which he ate. For some while he held a banana in his right hand. Then, quite suddenly, he peeled it roughly, rolled his eyes back in their sockets, threw back his head, flared his nostrils and, like some demented fruit bat, set about the thing with rapid-fire staccato lunges of startling ferocity. Mark was captivated. Four bananas disappeared in what seemed like a matter of seconds. Not satisfied with these he made a frenzied assault on an innocent mango, but the remaining contents of the fruit bowl were spared this terrible end by the advent of nightfall. In these latitudes it happened almost as rapidly as if someone had flipped a switch and now it was the signal for them to drift into the lounge - now doubling as the dining room - for dinner.

He was joined at his table by the Wanganui Debating Society and needless to say the conversation was less than sparkling. After about twenty pensive minutes during which they ate an unidentified soup like monks in meditation, Mr Wanganui, to Mark's complete surprise suddenly enquired whether he had ever tried wind surfing. Mark regretted that he had not. "Oh..." said Mr Wanganui "it's very popular in New Zealand."

"Really?" said Mark, trying to disguise his surprise and sound interested, "...and do you windsurf?" The man was seventy if he was a day so it seemed an odd question, it had just slipped out of his mouth. But in any case Mr Wanganui was already dormant again before the words had passed his lips.

Shortly after this the electricity failed. The night was impenetrably dark; Mark was quite literally unable to see his plate in front of him and could only form a picture of his surroundings through sound and touch. The mackintosh creaked somewhere over to his left and other noises told him the fruit bat was still enjoying his meal. The waitress, Lulu, appeared to be going about her business as if nothing was unusual. Perhaps it wasn't, but soon the inevitable happened and a dull thud told him she had hit the deck. A moment later and a glorious clatter gave him a rough idea of what had been on her tray. Undaunted, she went on with her work and after a while he heard a plate being placed in front of him. He could not see what was on it however and probed with his utensils in order to form a kind of radar picture of the meal.

At length the power was restored and this was the signal for a troupe of young men and women wearing garish floral lavalavas, grass skirts and garlands of frangipani and hibiscus flowers in their hair to pour into the room and set about entertaining the guests with a display of traditional songs and dances. This was called 'fia-fia' or 'fun-fun'. Mark had seen something similar at Aggie's Hotel, but while that show had been very slick and impressive and was topped by a bewitching fire dancer whirling round the pool, this lot appeared rougher and earthier and were probably, he thought, a bit closer to the authentic traditions. There was a distinct sense that they did this at home anyway on Saturday nights and had done since the dawn of time.

Mark was pleased, and just a little bit flustered, to see that one of the dancers was the very same beautiful young fisherman he had been staring at earlier out in the lagoon - and who had stared at him in the bar. Now he had a chance for an even closer look. Like the others, the young man wore only trunks and a grass skirt which parted slightly as it swirled offering tantalising glimpses of his strong, springy thighs. Mark could not take his eyes away. He was perhaps twenty or twenty-two, not more. He seemed to fizz with bottled energy and yet his movements were controlled and elegant. Inevitably they caught each other's eye and Mark realised immediately that the young man knew he had been watching him. He felt the blood surge in his face. 'Oh shit!' he thought, 'Oh shit, shit, shit!' He looked away in a rush of self-consciousness but his eyes went back as though on elastic. The young man was still looking straight at him, though his face gave nothing away. 'Oh Christ, oh shit, shit, shit, shit, shit!!! Whatever must he be thinking? Whatever is he going to do? Oh ... SHIT!' His heart was thumping in his chest. He took a long swallow of his beer and tried to feel grown up.

The dance - a Haka - came to a whirling stop amid general hoots and cheers and before Mark even knew what was happening the young man was at his side - actually sitting right there in the very next chair. He was panting a bit and sweating from his exertions, but his face was composed and calm. He looked straight at Mark and grinned. His eyes were enormous and shiny. He looked boyish yet at the same time there was something about him that was almost fatherly - protective.

"You Australian?"

He couldn't see the point in denying it. He was so relieved, not to say surprised that the guy's first words had not been 'why are you watching me, are you a poof?' that he just slipped even further off balance. He heard himself say "Yeah, that's right."

"I am Tofilau, but you can call me Tofi - everybody calls me Tofi."

"Hello Tofi, my name's Mark." They both nodded. He thought he had managed that pretty well, considering. His voice had been reasonably controlled even though inside he was sliding on ice. He had no idea what was happening, the only thing he was sure about was that he was definately not in control. But then they shook hands. Tofi's grip showed an animal strength that supported a silky sensitivity. It was a combination familiar to Mark from a hundred thousand daydreams but the physical reality of the contact went through his body like an electric shock.

"That girl there is Millie." Tofi indicated one of the dancers. "She is nice eh?"

"Yes, she's very nice" Mark agreed.

"She is my sister."

ark nodded and smiled but could think of no meaningful response. "That's nice" he said at last.

"You like her?" It was a question, but spoken like a pronouncement of truth.

"Yes Tofi, she's very beautiful." 'Oh no' he thought... 'oh shit!' Although he knew it was ridiculous he had allowed himself to think, just for a moment, that Tofi was actually chatting him up. But the little bubble of potential that had started to form in his mind had burst now; the slight frisson that accompanied it was just a passing shadow and all he wanted now was for the guy to go away.

"She look after you good tonight eh?"

He really couldn't be bothered now. But if nothing else at least he was back in control. He fixed the Samoan with his eyes, leaned back slightly, raised his eyebrows and tried what he thought was a wistful smile as he slowly shook his head. But the hoped for demurement did not come. Instead Tofi returned his gaze, his lovely eyes drilling and searching with unhurried confidence.

"So what is wrong with her?" He didn't seem offended. A faint smile crossed his face - or was that just Mark's imagination again?

"No, no, nothing's wrong with her Tofi, I just don't want to sleep with her, that's all."

"Okay. Perhaps then you like to sleep with me?" It didn't feel like an accusation and that surprised him more than anything else. The guy was so sanguine about it that he thought it was a joke at first. Again he had been thrown completely off balance and didn't really know what to think. But when he looked into Tofi's eyes he was in no doubt that the Samoan was serious. He must have been at least ten years younger, but those were the eyes of an older brother, smiling protectively down at him with the wisdom of experience yet full of boyish fun and physicality. He asked Mark what his room number was and he told him. Just like that. Without saying a word more Tofi leapt from the seat and re-joined his friends; it was time for another Haka.

Mark couldn't bear to stay in the lounge a moment longer. He went over to the bar and bought two bottles of beer then hurriedly escaped to the solitude and sanctuary of his room. He had a quick shower then sat on the balcony, shell-shocked, staring at the darkness. He couldn't quite believe that what had just happened had actually happened. Tofi wouldn't come - not really. But yes, he would! Of course he would - he really would! His mind raced and his pulse with it. He swallowed deep draughts of beer and tried to stay calm. 'He'll rob me. Oh my God that's it - he'll turn up with three mates and rob me - they'll take everything - my wallet - I'll be stranded! What if they rape me? They'll probably rape me and give me some awful disease!'

But while these voices jangled in his head they didn't actually bother him as much as he thought they should. He began to notice other things impressing themselves on him, calming him, reassuring him. The sound of the reef, constant in the distance, holding the ocean at bay, sealing in this little dreamworld, sealing in the serenity and shielding it from the outside. The air, so hot and still; it seemed to cushion and cradle him like a wonderful blanket. Just below the balcony was a large frangipani tree and the scent of it's flowers filled his nostrils and infused his body like an enveloping balm, driving other thoughts away, forcing him to focus on it's intense deliciousness.

It started to rain again. The music stopped over in the lounge. If Tofi was really going to come then it might be any time now. He knew that he ought to feel terrified, or at the very least profoundly anxious, but he didn't – he simply didn't.

Nine

Then it came - three taps on the door. He couldn't quite believe he had heard it, but there it was again, unmistakeable, three soft taps - tap - tap - tap - then a muffled voice "Mark ... Mark it's me Tofi, let me in."

He was across the room in a second and stood, intensely aware of the other man's presence behind the door. His head was clear, his breathing relaxed. He was not the same person he had been an hour before. He knew that something had happened to him - that some profound change had taken place in him. He felt like a child who had woken one day to find he was suddenly an adult. It was the strangest feeling; as though he had at last joined the human race, or had discovered that he was indeed real after all.

He opened the door. Tofilau stood before him, serene and sensual. He had changed his grass skirt for a lavalava and was naked from the waist up. He was soaking wet and vibrant as a racehorse. Mark's too casual "Hi" sounded ridiculous, but it didn't matter; their eyes were locked and he felt a rush of kinship and emotional solidarity wrapping itself around him, seeping into him, relaxing and reassuring him as though from the inside out.

He stepped to one side and Tofi came through into the room. Mark followed, studying the contours of his sinewy back as he walked. He had watched this man for so long and so intently today that the terrain of his body was already familiar to him, and yet he knew it remained a garden of delights waiting to be explored. And he would explore it. The knowledge - the certain knowledge - coursed in his veins like mother's milk. If all the good moments in his life were rolled up together into one they could not have equalled the goodness of this moment.

The rain, though a persistent presence, was now easing slightly, but it had done nothing to dispel the heat. The ceiling fan stirred the thick air a little, but not much. Mark had brought some bottles of mineral water from Apia and he took one from the fridge and offered it to Tofi. The Samoan said nothing, but grinned and kept his eyes on Mark while he swallowed down a generous draught. Mark studied the way his lips wrapped around the neck of the bottle; they were like his hands - firm and strong but at the same time supple and sensitive, controlling and caressing. He handed the bottle back to Mark who in turn put it to his lips. As he lifted his head to swallow, Tofi reached out and gently brushed his neck with the back of his fingers.

They went out onto the balcony where the rain, now heavier again, hung a gauze curtain just beyond the rail. The air lay still around them, warm and very wet. The light from the room made little headway into the night, just managing to suffuse the balcony with a gentle, creamy haze. Two deck chairs, the kind with wooden arms and old, musty canvas seats, were placed side by side. The two men sat down and Tofi immediately took Mark's right leg, lifted it and placed it over the arms of the chairs so that his legs were partly splayed and his heel rested in the Samoan's lap. He held Mark's knee firmly with his right hand while with his left he began tracing feather-light circles up and down his thigh.

The suddenness of his action took Mark by surprise, but his hands did far more than reassure. Mark quickly found himself becoming acutely aware of every part of his body. It was as though some current had been switched on. His whole skin felt sensitized and his body seemed to be humming. The sensation as Tofi trailed his fingers around his ticklish inner thigh was a fine balance between pleasure and a delicate pain. One minute Tofi was raking his fingernails over the skin, the next he was brushing so very gently over the hairs. Then he would dig his fingers in and knead the flesh, exploring, discovering, taking possession.

Mark was sitting still in the chair, but his body was buzzing and he couldn't remember ever having felt quite so alive before. His cock was so full and hard he thought it might burst and it strained painfully against the cotton of his boxer shorts, which were all he was wearing. Tofi had to have seen it, he thought. He couldn't very well have failed to notice, but Mark didn't care, he wanted him to see, he wanted to be naked so that Tofi could see every part of him. Every time the Samoan's fingers travelled down his thigh, inching closer with each pass to that most private of places, Mark feared that he might faint dead away just from the sheer pleasure of it. Then Tofi's fingers began to linger around the rim of the fabric, brushing back and forth, lifting the edge slightly and creeping under - half an inch - a little more. He found the crease between Mark's thigh and cheek and lingered there, probing, stroking, enjoying the contours and textures of the flesh and just letting Mark feel him there, so close to his very fundament. Finally the insistent fingers brushed the side of his scrotum and poor old Mark practically jumped into the sea. Tofi laughed and did it again, with a gossamer touch. He leaned nearer and whispered in Mark's ear: "You like that?" It wasn't really a question, but by now Mark was incapable of answering anyway, even if he had had anything coherent to say.

Tofi's other hand had all this time been holding Mark's knee firmly across the arm of the chair, but now he brought it down and hooked a finger into the waistband of his shorts. With his left hand he continued to stroke, ever so gently, just under Mark's testicles. Mark's cock, throbbing away in it's cotton prison was by now issuing copious amounts of sweet moisture. Tofi lifted the elastic, just a little, and peeked inside. Instantly Mark sat forward so as to cover himself. Poised on the brink of this intimate little surrender he was suddenly overcome with shyness, or at least with a desire for shyness. He wasn't really coy, but he desperately wanted to be. He felt the exquisite little pain of that most intimate of moments and he wanted it to go on for ever.

Tofi brushed his knuckles to and fro over Mark's stomach. "Mark" he said quietly, "there's no need to be shy with me." Again he could not answer, he was far beyond speaking. Tofi leaned in close and brushed his nose against Mark's ear. Mark could feel the hot breath against his face. He spoke slowly in a sonorous voice that was almost a whisper: "We are both boys Mark, we are both boys." Mark nearly came as he heard those words. "Come on, let me see you. Let me take your shorts off and have a good look at you." Mark sat back. Tofi moved from his chair and knelt in front of him, grinning joyously and humming to himself. He lifted the waistband of Mark's shorts and slipped them off. Almost in the same movement he stood back and sat up on the rail of the balcony. He used his feet to push Mark's legs wide apart over the arms of the chair and with a huge grin and a contented sigh he said: "Now then, let's have a g-o-o-d look at my little white boy."

For a while he did just that, letting his eyes rove slowly around Mark's body as he sprawled happily before him. Then, pinning his right leg with one foot, he began to rake the other up and down his left thigh in long, slow sweeps, much as he had done earlier with his fingers. Soon he was exploring Mark's groin with his big toe. All his movements were slow and deliberate, taking his time, enjoying himself.

Using his big toe he began moving Mark's balls around playfully, first one, then the other, sliding them about in their spongy sack and examining their contours. He pinned one with his foot and squeezed it gently, his eyes moving back and forth from Mark's face to his groin as he studied his reactions closely. He increased the pressure a little, causing Mark to catch his breath and wriggle slightly. Tofi's grin widened and grew smirky. He loved watching him squirm like that and chuckled as he kept the torture going.　After a while he released the poor testicle, but immediately trapped the other one and repeated the little torment.

At length he relented and started to slide his toe up and down the length of Mark's rigid cock.　Pausing at the head he said "Let me see now, I believe I'll just pull this skin back." Mark had always thought that this should properly be done very slowly.　This most private and fundamental part of a man was also such a very beautiful thing, round and purple like a lovely ripe plum.　To peel it was to peel fruit, slowly revealing the vulnerable, sensitive flesh with anticipation and infinite pleasure.　Tofi went about it now with a reverence that was flattering and betrayed a rare sensitivity.　Mark's final surrender was now complete and he gazed up at Tofi, helpless and ecstatic.　The young Samoan was now his brother, his soul mate, his flesh mate, his torturer and Mark was utterly his.

His cock stood straight out away from his stomach and the swollen head strained painfully as it pressed against Tofi's foot. Tofi ran his toe all over the cock head, now scraping with the nail, now rubbing in little circles with the pad.　He went about this with rapt concentration and rejoiced in the reactions he provoked as Mark squirmed about in the chair.　He particularly relished the acute sensitivity he seemed to find around and under the rim so he focussed his attention there, sliding his toe around and around until finally Mark could stand it no longer.　Seeing that he was obviously close to bursting, Tofi laughed and said "Yes boy, now I'm going to watch you come - I'm going to watch you."　With that a long white string leapt from Mark's cock and went clean past his shoulder.　A second traced an arc in the night air and plopped onto his chest, then a whole series of smaller pulses spattered around his navel. His cock continued to strain against Tofi's foot long after he was spent and the Samoan loved to watch it and to feel it's little throbs.　Tofi was laughing and cheering: "You white boy, you got plenty juice in them balls.　Yessir, you my juicy little boy that's for sure."

Mark had never ejaculated like that before - so painfully, so ecstatically or so copiously, but then he had never ejaculated in front of anyone before. Physically he was exhausted but mentally so alive. The sheer rapture of that moment was something he had never ever known before. This was more pleasure than he had realised it was possible to experience, more than he could really take in. Tofi danced off into the room and emerged with a roll of toilet tissue. He knelt down and mopped Mark's torso as he lay limply in the chair. When he was done he produced a bottle of water that he had taken from the fridge. He unscrewed the cap and slowly drizzled a thin stream of freezing water over Mark's face, into his mouth, down his neck, over his nipples, down to his navel, then directly over the still more or less erect cock head, along the length of his shaft and finally over his testicles. He loved to watch the fleshy sack curling and contracting, rolling the balls lugubriously as the water trickled over them, and he kept this up for a long time. Then, quite suddenly, Mark burst into tears.

It was a bigger surprise to him than it was to Tofi, but he couldn't stop to think about it, all he could do was sob and sob and boy did it feel good! Tofi slid a protective arm around his shoulder and drew him closer, then put a hand to his chin and gently turned his face. Tofi's face in turn was calm, his smile radiant. His beautiful eyes were shiny, drawing Mark in, soothing and supporting him. Mark was a child again, lost and found, and he snuggled into the cradle of Tofi's arms while his tears slowly subsided.

"Mark," said Tofi at last, "you never do this before do you? You never play these games with anyone before." Mark did not answer, he just lay there limply, resting his head on Tofi's shoulder. "That is so sweet" said Tofi. "You are a rich man, you go all around the world in aeroplanes. Me, I never been anywhere, only sometimes to Apia and once to Pago with my father. But here we are - you are my little boy now I think - I teach you big things tonight yes? Big things."

A weak "Yes Tofi" was all Mark could manage to utter. He had stopped crying by now and the two sat, snuggling and nuzzling, comfortable in each other's warmth. Mark thought that he would never get used to it - the strength, the tenderness, the warmth, the kinship, the constant shock of the simplest physical contact. It was all so ... so ... well, so bloody fantastic. He would never get used to it and he would never, ever, ever take it for granted.

"So..." Tofi spoke in that half question, half assertion way of his. "You want to see me?"

"Oh yes ... yes Tofi, I want to see you." He was aware of an enormous sense of privilege and the weight of it made his voice quiver. Tofi kept an arm around his shoulder but drew back slightly and regarded him with another of his big smirky grins. He toyed with Mark's nose and said "Okay, but just remember - I'm still boss man here." With that he reached down, untied the front of his lavalava, slipped it off and tossed it into the room. Almost in the same motion he stood and moved back to his position by the balcony rail. Mark had half expected him to be naked under his wrap-around but instead he was wearing white briefs of a thin and flimsy cotton that was itself wet where his lavalava had soaked through in the rain. The bulge they contained was wonderful, round and full, it looked as though he had a tennis ball down there with a saveloy curled around it and where the wet fabric clung to him Mark could clearly see the nut-brown flesh itself.

He sat up on the rail with his feet tucked under and his legs wide apart. Still grinning he said "Kneel here" and pointed to the floor in front of him. Mark did as he was told, and finding himself suddenly surrounded by powerful thighs and with his face so close to the very quick of the man he was again moved far beyond words by the immediacy and intensity of Tofi's physical presence. Tofi stroked his hair with both hands and played with his ears. Gently but firmly he directed Mark's face against his thigh where his mouth found smooth, warm skin stretched over muscles that quivered with energy and life. Mark was lost again - drowning contentedly in male flesh. This beautiful man had let him in, and while he was still struggling to believe that it was all really happening, his sense of gratitude was so deep it was almost worshipful.

Mark found his head being steered closer to the most private place. Soon he was exploring sensuous curves and bulges; his lips and tongue travelling over the wet cotton, discovering the contours, the sweet and musky aroma, the springy texture of the genital flesh. Tofi's testicles were big, as big as plums, and Mark loved the way they slid around in their spongy sack. He used his nose to play with them, then his tongue - pressing it against one globe until it eased off to the side, then collecting it and repeating the game, over and over. Tofi's hand came down in front and he lifted the leg of his briefs about an inch or two - just enough to offer a tantalising glimpse of his scrotum. The crease of his groin, the curling brown skin, the weight and presence of his testicle - the pleasure and anticipation were together unbearable and Mark wished that he could freeze that moment in time - that he could make it go on for ever and ever.

At length Tofi pushed him back a little, brought his legs down and slipped his briefs down and off, straight away resuming his position on the rail. Mark was like a fox caught in headlights. He was transfixed. All he could do was stare and stare, thinking that there could surely be nothing more perfect in the world than the sight of this man sitting there like that, naked.

Tofi's cock was not yet fully erect and it lolled heavily against his thigh, slowly filling with lovely little throbs and pulses. Without waiting to be told, Mark pressed his mouth against it's base and moved slowly along the shaft, exploring with his lips, considering it's contours, feeling it's heat. The circumcised head was magnificent - crimson and full - and he ran his tongue over and around it as though it were a skinned peach - vulnerable - sensitive - delicious. He took the whole head in his mouth - just the head - and let it sit there for a long time, feeling it's weight on his tongue, letting the aroma permeate his nose and throat. Tofi cradled Mark's head in his hands and eased himself further inside. Mark had often practised this using bananas and had always managed to gag and choke, but for some reason this was much more comfortable, although his mouth was wide open and Tofi's cock completely filled it. Tofi kept saying - "That's it ... just relax..." and he did. He wanted him there so much, inside him, filling him up. Tofi held the back of his head firmly with one hand while with the other he stroked and played with his ear. He began to rock back and forth in a steady motion, his cock head now grazing on Mark's teeth, now sliding slowly but deeply inside until his face was pressed into the bush of wiry black hairs. Mark was somewhere he had never been before. He was a child again, wide-eyed in wonderland, adrift in a great inner space of pure and absolute pleasure. Time was gone. Everything was gone. All that existed now was his mouth and Tofi's flesh. Male flesh. Vibrant, aromatic and sensuous, it was a warm sea enveloping him and he swam joyfully in it.

He had no idea how long it went on, but at length Tofi's body stiffened and quivered and he let out a huge groan. He pulled right out and immediately his juice hit Mark full in the face, hot and creamy. Mark loved it. Tofi gripped his hair and pulled his head back as pulse after pulse covered his face, ran down his neck, ran into the corners of his mouth. When at last Tofi was spent he lay his cock across Mark's face. It was slippery and still rigid and he slid it around, smearing his juice everywhere. He kept this up for ages while it slowly let itself down, until at last it was a spongy thing again, warm and heavy across Mark's lips.

They stayed like that for a long time, neither of them

attempting to move. Mark felt Tofi's essence laying over him like a benediction, infusing him with every breath he took. He was completely at peace, for the first time in his life at one with another man and he could happily have remained kneeling there for the rest of eternity.

It was Tofi who broke the spell, though he did so very gently. In a quiet voice he said "Look at you, you're such a mess. Go and clean yourself up." Mark went to the bathroom and wiped his face with tissues then washed it. When he came back Tofi was sprawled on the bed and he patted the mattress, indicating that Mark should join him. Mark lay on his back and Tofi rolled over, half covering him and with one leg wedged between his. They wriggled a bit so as to snuggle deeply in and Tofi was soon asleep. Mark lay awake for a long time, thinking of nothing but the slow rhythm of the other man's breathing and the warm presence of his body wrapped around him.

Eventually he drifted off and the next thing he knew it was daylight and his friend was no longer beside him. Rubbing the sleep from his eyes he looked through the door and saw him standing on the balcony, naked, gazing out at the sea. He called out and Tofi turned and smiled then leaned back against the rail and stretched gloriously. His lavalava was draped over the rail beside him and Mark watched as he first pulled on his briefs then wrapped the long sheet around his waist and knotted it in front. As he came back into the room Mark sat up and, feeling suddenly aware of his nakedness, pulled the sheet around himself. Tofi laughed and straight away pulled it off again then sat on the bed and ran his hand all over Mark's body, paying no attention however to his cock, which had sprung quickly to life. Instead he pulled him in close and they held each other in a long, long cuddle. Finally Tofi kissed him on the cheek. "Mark, I have to go now. But I come back tonight yes? Ten-o-clock?"

"Oh yes ... please come back."

"You like that?"

"Yes Tofi, I'd like that very much. Very much."

Tofi laughed. "Maybe I teach you some more things. Maybe I bring some things to play with." A little flicker went through Mark - whether of fear or excitement, or both, he wasn't sure.

"Things? What sort of things Tofi?"

The Samoan laughed again and the old conspiratorial grin lit up his face. "You'll see" he said, "we have fun tonight I think, we play some games tonight." He kissed Mark again and was gone.

Mark lay back on the bed and stretched himself, tensing and relaxing his muscles, luxuriating in his limbs, marvelling at the new found possibilities of his skin and sinews. Years of solitary play had given him great insights into the sensitivities of his genitals, but out of the blue, in one evening that knowledge had been opened out over his entire body. Tofi had switched on a light and Mark, at long, long last, had woken up.

Ravenously hungry, he jumped out of bed and into the shower, threw on a tee-shirt and some shorts and danced his way over to the dining room. When Lulu came over, smiling, to take his order he felt certain she would straight away know what he had been up to the night before. Quite how she would have known he wasn't really sure but it seemed impossible that you could have an experience like that without it being obvious to everyone around you. Not that he cared. He understood now, perhaps really for the first time, that the world was full of sexual people and he was at last one of them, no longer on the outside, never again on the outside.

He ordered corned beef hash and fried eggs and preceded this with a bowl of sliced mango. The pink flesh was as fresh as could be and ridiculously sweet and juicy. He couldn't put the pieces in his mouth without flashing on the events of last night or feeling a stirring in his groin. The hash was delicious, made with yams instead of potato and piled high on the plate. He washed it down with a large mug of coffee, then took a second mug and sat contentedly on the verandah, gazing out through a frame of palm trees at the shimmering lagoon, the reef and the endless blue beyond

But the sky began to cloud over and within minutes it was raining again. The reef disappeared and in a matter of minutes the beach, not fifty metres away, was also hidden from view as the rain became a fizzing haze in front of him. He listened to it drumming on the corrugated iron roof. The air remained as hot as ever, just growing thicker and wetter around him. He had no real plans for today and thought he might just as well sit here and stare at the rain. Not that there was really very much else to do. But he loved it - he loved this rain with it's warmth and it's strength and it's hypnotic drumming. All his life he had known only cold, feeble, miserable rain, but here in Samoa he had found something entirely different - rain that was hot and deep - rain that nourished him, that made him feel serene, elated. It surrounded him like a womb of wetness - warm, sustaining and spectacular and it felt like the centre of all life. He sprawled and was lost in it.

But as well as the drumming of the rain on the roof he heard something else. Those little voices that had been so easily brushed aside last night. He still didn't know quite how it had happened - it was just the place - the place itself had changed him, had somehow done what years of rationalising and lectures from Phyllis had never achieved. But they were still there, those voices, out there somewhere - 'Who was Tofi anyway? What were his motives in all this? Was he working? Has he robbed me? Will I pick up some awful disease?' But while these questions flickered in his head none of them truly bothered him. He felt impervious, as though he were secure in this fantastic little dreamworld and they were outside somewhere, no longer able to control him, no longer able to stop him joining in. Tension and inhibition belonged to his old self and the recollection of those demons was like the memory of a bad dream. The air of this place had penetrated his bones. He had lost the capacity to feel tense, it had been leeched out of him by the heat, dissolved in the damp air and washed away by the rain. He felt clean now - clean and alive.

Ten

Mr Wanganui might have been quite a looker at one time, thought Mark. His body now showed the first decayings of early old age, the slightly crumpled posture, the slowness of movement, the skin beginning to wrinkle and sag a little. But his eyes were still bright, his jaw strong and his features pleasantly in proportion. His dimpled cheeks still retained a little of the sinew that had once made his face defined and purposeful. Yeah - thirty, even twenty years ago he was definitely a cutie.

Mark had again found himself seated with them at dinner and the three sat in dour silence. The Wanganui's ate their food with a measure of solemnity as though it were a dull but necessary chore. Why, Mark wondered, had they come to this place if they were going to be so miserable all the time? How could they find so little pleasure in life? If this was them on holiday then what ever must they be like back at home? He amused himself with images of Wanganui as as strange, unearthly place with zombies shuffling slowly about in the streets - mainly in an attempt to take his mind off the pleasures that awaited him later. He was like a child waiting for Christmas morning and the anticipation was almost more than he could bear.

He finished his meal. He had tried to take time over it as there were still a couple of hours to kill before his rendezvous with Tofi, but with no conversation to help it was difficult to drag things out very much. He ordered a cup of coffee and when it came he lingered over it so that it was cold before he had finished it. Then he ordered another. No matter how hard he tried to focus his mind on other things it was hopeless - the instant his tongue pressed against the rim of the cup and the warm liquid touched his lips there was a stirring in his groin.

Although his shorts were quite baggy he felt sure he would not be able to escape from the restaurant without someone noticing. Dinner had been impossible. As he opened his mouth to receive succulent pieces of chicken breast or broke off some baked banana to mop up the juice he was constantly reminded of the pleasures of last night. The whole world seemed to be comprised of nothing but sensuality and eroticism. Everything seemed erotic, everything around him and everything he could think of. He couldn't look at anything without a possible sexual use for it jumping into his mind. The bottle of mineral water on the table was a vivid echo of last night. His brown, sunburnt arm against the white of the table cloth. The verandah rail outside, so similar in design to that on his balcony where Tofi had sat. The music playing in the bar was the same Polynesian singing that had wafted over as he waited for Tofi to come. Finally he decided it was hopeless. If he could get up from the table and exit the room without his mother spotting that he had an erection then he could certainly escape from the Wanganui Debating Society.

He very nearly spat a mouthful of coffee out as the memory struck him. He hadn't thought of that singular difficulty in twenty years but the recollection swam into his mind from nowhere, sudden and vivid. His cheeks flushed and his sphincter tightened and tingled.

When Mark was twelve the school summer holiday was an endless round of sunny days and carefree play. Together with his friend Robert he would spend most of his time whizzing round country lanes on his bike or huddled in Robert's partly converted loft making plastic model aeroplanes or pouring over the latest issue of Flight Magazine. But once a week, on a Thursday, Robert's mother had to go to work in the afternoon and his brother Steve, who was sixteen, was charged with looking after him. Steve, however, had other ideas and would instead disappear out with his mates, leaving Robert with the house to himself for a couple of hours.

The two boys were quick to appreciate the potential of this situation - once a week, from two to four in the afternoon they had an opportunity to get up to absolutely anything they wanted, with no possibility of anyone ever finding out. Although they were both just about on the fringes of puberty and knew nothing, as yet, of masturbation, orgasms or any such thing, they were both nevertheless frantically horny.

It began as a game where they took it in turns - one was the Nazi interrogator while the other was the prisoner. The prisoner was required to strip naked and lie on the bed whereupon he was ruthlessly tickled and his genitals roughly handled in an 'interrogation' that could last anything from five minutes to half an hour depending on how cruel the interrogator was feeling or how long the prisoner could stand it. They quickly established however that Robert was much happier being the torturer while Mark was far more interested in being the victim. Both boys were excrutiatingly ticklish, but while Robert could stand it for only a short while, Mark could happily have lain there all day while his friend's fingers played over his body.

It was never certain until the last minute that Steve would go out and leave his brother. Mrs Jarvis didn't leave the house until one thirty and was home again three hours later. She waited across the road for her bus and Steve had to wait until he had seen her actually get on before he knew it was safe for him to leave. The minute he did so Robert would be on the phone to Mark..."All clear, come on over."

"I'm just finishing my lunch. Give me fifteen minutes."

"Okay, but not a minute more. Don't you dare be late."

Mark was always in the middle of lunch when the call came. As soon as he had put the receiver down he would have hot cheeks and a raging hard-on. On the very threshold of puberty it was already large enough to show in his trousers and his problem now was how to return to the dining room, where his mother sat at the table, and finish his dinner without doing anything to make her suspicious. He developed a strategy of pretending to carry on the conversation after Robert had hung up. This gave him time to concentrate on something other than the afternoon's anticipated pleasures so that his willy would behave itself and he could at least avoid the unthinkable horror of his mother noticing it.

"Was that Robert?" she would ask as he came back to the table.

"Yes." Mark had to work very hard to appear nonchalant. He couldn't allow his voice to show any hint of excitement or his manner to give any clue that the activities they planned that afternoon were so far from innocent. "Yes" he would say. "Mrs Jarvis has gone to work but Steve's there. We're going to play football in the garden."

"Well make sure you're back by five-o-clock for tea and do be careful cycling up that road."

"I will" he would chirp. But now he had the problem of getting up from the table, beneath which his willy was again seriously misbehaving itself. But necessity was always the mother of invention and he quickly mastered a technique of turning away from her as he bent and pushed his chair back, while giving no hint of the discomfort he caused himself.

As he pedalled furiously round to Robert's house, half-a-mile away, his swollen crotch would rock about on the saddle; he always loved the sensation and would grind himself in as hard as he could as he toiled up the hill. Once there the routine was always the same. He would let himself in the back door and go to the foot of the stairs. Robert would be waiting at the top. "Ah" he would shout, "the prisoner is here at last. Get up here now."

Whilst everything they did together was physically harmless, Robert, once established in his role as the torturer, had shown himself to be wonderfully creative. When it came to exposing and exploiting Mark's vulnerabilities he was on a steep learning curve, such that with each session their games grew increasingly intense. One of his early discoveries was that

Mark's feeling of nakedness was greatly enhanced if he had no access to his clothes. Thus he would make Mark strip on the landing and climb the loft ladder stark naked. Following him up he would draw the ladder up and secure the trap door, leaving the clothes behind. Sometimes he would send Mark downstairs with no clothes on and with a task to complete, such as to make them a drink or to locate various items hidden about the house. There would always be a strict time limit and a forfeit to pay if he didn't make it back in time.

In another game Robert would sit and watch while he made Mark do jobs such as vacuuming the carpet or washing the dishes, always stark naked, and would make endless comments about how silly he looked or how his willy boinged around. Then he would take the vacuum cleaner and press the nozzle against Mark's balls or put it over the end of his willy and make the skin vibrate. Back in the attic Mark would find himself with his wrists tied to a beam above his head and Robert would spend ages tickling him. He quickly discovered Mark's most sensitive places and accordingly gave these particular attention. He also refined his techniques, using a range of methods from digging vigorously into his ribs to brushing up and down with feather-light strokes.

Mark's genitals naturally received the greatest attention. His foreskin would be stretched cruelly, both forwards and backwards. Once held firmly back, the end of his willy would be rubbed with a dry flannel or stroked with fingernails. Sometimes Robert would even put tiny strips of Sellotape on it and peel them off at varying speeds. 'Quiztime' meant that one end of a pyjama cord was tied around his genitals and the other end tied to a sandcastle bucket which was then allowed to hang between his legs. Robert would sit on a stool in front of him with *The Golden Treasury of Knowledge* open on his lap and would ask him questions. Everytime he got an answer wrong, or didn't know it, Robert placed a marble in the bucket. Mark's general knowledge was pretty good, but even so it was never long before he was unable to stand it and he would beg his friend to untie the bucket. But Robert would only free him from this torment once he had agreed to be his total and absolute slave and to obey any commands he was given for the rest of the afternoon.

One such trial was often to lick Robert's willy. Robert always found this a hilarious idea and went under the cheerful misapprehension that Mark disliked it. In fact he loved to get on his knees and have Robert take his willy out and place it in his mouth, then to have to lick it thoroughly, paying close attention to his friend's instructions. His enjoyment was only slightly marred by having to pretend not to like it - if he let on that he actually enjoyed it there was a danger that Robert would find something else to make him do instead.

On one occasion, when Mark was happily trussed up in the loft and Robert was rolling his balls with one hand and tickling his ribs with the other, they heard the back door close. They both froze. Steve was home, unexpectedly early. Fortunately for them Robert had left the loft ladder down and in one brilliant, panic-stricken movement he shot down it, grabbed Mark's clothes, shot back up, hauled up the ladder and shut the trap door. Steve called out to them and Robert answered, trying to keep control of his voice while his breathing was desperately short. He untied his friend, who got hurriedly dressed. Scarcely thinking what they were doing they flew around the table, trying to make it look as much as possible as if they had been quietly working on a model aeroplane. Their secret world had come perilously close to being discovered and the shock was enormous. Part of the attraction of all these games was the acute sense they both shared of just how naughty it all was. The consequences of being found out were unthinkable and their greatest fear was of the embarrassment, which would be overwhelming, unbearable and utterly unavoidable. They had escaped this time, but the shock had greatly unsettled them both.

But for Mark it also did something else. It sparked off the pleasant and enduring little fantasy that Steve had indeed caught them and far from blowing the whistle, had actually joined in. Mark had this vague idea that Steve, being sixteen, would know all sorts of things that they didn't yet and he would be able to teach them. He wasn't sure just what things these might be exactly, but he was certain there were things, to do with willies and stuff, that an older boy would be able to explain, or better still to demonstrate. He was also very taken with the idea of being tormented and played with by Robert and Steve together. He didn't make very much sense of this, he just knew that it was a bloody exciting idea and it didn't half make his willy go stiff.

One day when he was round at Robert's he caught a glimpse, by pure chance, of Steve getting out of the bath. He had never even seen his own father - not that he could remember anyway, his wasn't really that sort of family - and this was the first time he had had proper sight of a naked man. It was only the briefest of glimpses as he happened to run past the door, but it was a defining moment in his twelve year old life. For Steve had what appeared in that instant to be a medium sized squirrel bouncing around between his legs. In that short but intense moment Mark was electrified and his brain managed to register a huge amount of information. He saw the sinewy, athletic thighs with their coating of fluffy hair. He saw the flat, strong stomach and the little band of hair running down from the navel to spread and become a thick bush. He saw the vein standing out along the shaft of Steve's willy, the roundness and particular shape of the head, the fullness of the balls. He sensed the springy texture of the genital flesh. In the blink of an eye he took all this in and the shock went through him like a bolt of lightning. He was infinitely curious and consumed with a desire for ... what? He wasn't really sure. Some sort of closeness, as yet undefined; a need to be in some way connected to this fascinating body.

He wanted to have an exclusive and secret link with Steve. He wanted Steve to teach him things - extremely private things about willies and balls and men's bodies. In his favourite fantasy the two of them would go away camping together. They would pitch their tent in some remote wood and there spend all day climbing trees and wrestling. Then at night they would snuggle down together in the tent and Steve would tell him and show him all kinds of wonderful things - things that only boys knew about. The next day Steve would tie him to a tree, naked of course, and spend the whole day subjecting him to playful and exquisite torments. And they would pass a whole week like that, or maybe even two, hidden away in their own secret and intimate little world of maleness.

The following spring Mr Jarvis got another job and the whole family moved away up north somewhere. Mark and Robert exchanged letters for a while, but it wasn't long before they lost touch and Steve had been replaced in Mark's affections, now that he was at grammar school, by a whole succession of athletic sixth formers and a number of young male teachers.

He was finally startled out of his Proustian reverie by Lulu, who came over and asked if he wanted anything else. He ordered a couple of beers to take to his room. When she brought them he rose from the table, putting his left hand in his pocket as he did so to make a reasonable tent, dangled the beers as casually as he could in front of his fly and walked confidently out of the dining room. The instant he was off the verandah and onto the path the darkness seized and swallowed him and he knew he was safe. It took a moment for his eyes to adjust and he stepped gingerly, although he knew the path well by now. But walking seemed to help with his general circulation and his tumescence subsided a little. It also served to clear his head - picking his way along in the dark proved to be the best distraction he had had all evening and he quickly realised that this was the solution to the problem of getting through the next hour.

He went to his room and put the beers in the fridge. He changed his shirt and shorts for a pair of boxers. He took one of the beers, left his key under the mat and went out onto the beach. He wandered slowly along to the far end and back, not really aware of much except the texture of the sand under his toes and the warm air coiling around him as he moved. At length he stopped, sat down at the edge of the lagoon and slid his feet in. The water was dark and still and the warmth of it was a constant surprise. He inched further in until his shorts were wet and the water lapped gently around his testicles. He loved the sensation of this and sat still for a few minutes, enjoying it. But he couldn't resist the sea and, putting his now empty beer down, eased himself slowly into the fabulous bath. The only sound was the rustling of sand beneath him. The warm water was glassy-smooth and luscious and it slid creamily around his body. And there was a movement in the water - slight but discernible - a rising and falling, slow and subtle like the breathing of a sleeping man.

He floated with no effort at all and after a long time - he didn't know how long - he realised that he was in danger of falling asleep. As he emerged from the sea another thought crossed his mind and with it something that might have been close to concern if he had not been in such a mellow state - that he had stayed in too long and had missed Tofi. He hurried back to his room. The key was still under the mat where he had left it. The idea of time being important seemed rather alien - jarring - like a memory of real life breaking into a pleasant dream. But his clock said half past nine, so with a measure of relief he had a shower, put on a fresh pair of boxers, took the other beer from the fridge and sat down on the balcony.

The warm air condensed around the cold glass bottle which quickly became very wet and dripped cold spots onto his legs. This brought more memories of last night and he felt a stirring in his groin in response. The neck of the bottle grew slippery and his fingers began to play over it. He put his lips around it and took a long swallow. But just at that moment he heard it again - three soft taps on the door and Tofi's whispered voice:

"Mark ... Mark it's me Tofi ... let me in."

He stood, turned and stared at the door. Smiling, he raised the bottle and took another pull, savouring the moment.

"Mark" a note of urgency now in Tofi's voice.

"Okay, I'm just coming."

His erection had subsided slightly as he stood up but it was still obvious, even though his boxers were quite baggy, and he didn't want to open the door like that so on the way he grabbed a towel and wrapped it around his waist.

Tofi emerged from the darkness outside into the half-light of the room carrying one of those bags Mark had seen that were made from plaited pandanus leaves. He took Mark's beer from him without saying a word, walked over to the bed, put his bag down, swallowed the rest of the beer and stood looking at his friend with a huge smirky grin on his face.

"Lock the door" he ordered. Mark did as he was told, his heart pounding in his chest. As he turned back to the room he saw Tofi throw off his lavalava and jump onto the bed. Once again he felt the shock of being suddenly confronted with this perfect, athletic body; so strong, he thought, and chiselled and vibrant and ... well just downright fucking beautiful. Tofi's briefs were startlingly white against his coppery skin. As he sprawled luxuriously on the bed so the thin fabric stretched over the glorious curves and bulges, now and then lifting at the edges to allow glimpses of the dark, curling, secret flesh. Mark was melting.

Tofi knelt up on the edge of the bed and told him to come closer. He reached out, pulled the towel away and threw it over a chair. Immediately he ran his hands round the back of Mark's thighs, up the legs of his boxers and over his cheeks. The suddenness of this intimate contact was thrilling and a surprise after the gentleness of his approach last night. His hands were sensitive but insistent as they moved over Mark's skin, travelling around his hips and over the front of his thighs. Mark stood still with his hands by his side while Tofi explored him, with each passing moment feeling more and more like a little boy. But his erection was manly enough and while it strained against the cotton Tofi was careful to ignore it completely.

After many minutes Tofi took one hand out from under Mark's shorts, hooked a finger into the waistband and stretched it out to it's furthest extent before letting it go. It stung as it slapped against his stomach and made him flinch slightly. Tofi grinned and stretched it out again, but this time he deliberately held it open, leaving the very tip of Mark's cock exposed and just visible. Although the door to the balcony was open the air in the room was warm and soggy and they both felt it slide over their bodies as the ceiling fan slowly turned. Standing there with his boxers held open Mark could feel the air moving around his groin. He knew that Tofi could just see the tip of him and this inevitably swelled even more and rose slightly. Tofi brushed the tip of his forefinger across the slit. "Mine" he said "...mine to play with." Never in his life before had Mark felt quite so naked, so exquisitely vulnerable. It was an extraordinary moment and again he would have given any- thing to have been able to freeze it in time. He thought it had gone when the elastic stung him again, but straight away Tofi instructed him to remove his shorts. He had to bend slightly in order to do this - their faces came very close and he felt warm breath against his cheek. Tofi brought a hand up and caressed his face, toying with one ear lobe and nibbling the other. He held him like that as his shorts fell to the floor and he stepped out of them. Then Tofi whispered in his ear - "You're my boy aren't you? Stand up straight and let daddy have a good look."

As soon as he did so Tofi's hands moved purposefully up his legs. One resumed it's exploration of his bum cheeks while a single finger brushed delicately at the base of his crotch. He lifted each testicle in turn, appreciating it's weight, then traced gossamer circles around his scrotum causing the skin to curl and the flesh to tighten slightly into a round and spongy purse. He traced a finger very slowly up the length of Mark's erection and as he brought it down again he pressed a little harder so that the foreskin was peeled back with it. He continued to slide his finger gently up and down the shaft and Mark found himself helplessly oozing beads of glistening precum. Tofi began to scoop these and to rub them all over the swollen plum. Soon he was using all his fingers, digging, kneading and raking Mark's cockhead with studied pleasure. Mark, while twisting and gasping under this playful torment managed nevertheless to keep his hands firmly by his sides in a determined gesture of schoolboy submission.

After amusing himself like this for a very long time Tofi at last turned his attention to Mark's testicles. He loved the spongy texture of the sack and the glutinous movements of the tender, slippery globes within. He squeezed them together testingly and Mark's reactions confirmed what he had suspected last night - that this particular sensation affected him in some curiously fundamental way. A perfect balance of pain and pleasure, and with skilful judgment Tofi could tread the finest of lines between them.

He edged back into the middle of the bed and by maintaining his hold on Mark's balls, forced him to follow. When they were kneeling face to face and very close together Tofi put an arm around Mark's lower back and indicated that he should rock gently back and forth. With his other hand he cupped Mark's balls in his palm so that as he rocked forward they were squeezed slightly and as he rocked back he found relief. Pain - relief - pain - relief - an easy rhythm was established and with it came a new level of intimacy that was, for Mark, extreme and over-whelming.

He tipped his head back and Tofi kissed his neck. The

Samoan's mouth felt strong but his lips were silky and sensitive and his breath urgent and hot. He ran his mouth all over Mark's neck and soon they were kissing. For all they had been through together this was the first time they had really kissed properly and for Mark it was like eating fruit - only a thousand times more pleasurable. Tofi's tongue was hard and slippery and it probed his mouth with a confident, leisurely insistence while all the time the rhythmic massaging of his testicles continued. Tofi leaned his head back and Mark was able to let his mouth wander over the landscape of his muscular neck and appreciate once again the warm skin and lively, succulent sinew beneath.

It was Tofi who finally broke the spell. "Mark" he said, in a quiet voice "...don't you want to know what I've got in the bag?" Mark didn't answer - he didn't have to. Tofi's lovely doe-eyes had a boyish twinkle in them, but he saw everything - Mark was an open book to him, displayed and helpless. If he had any residual fears about what the bag might contain they just added piquancy to his desperate excitement. He couldn't have stopped now even if he had wanted to. Tofi could do anything to him that he wanted and they both knew it.

Tofi reached into the bag, which was on the floor beside the bed, rummaged around a bit, then drew out a length of rough cord. "Hold out your wrists." As he gave the instruction the corners of his mouth curled into a restrained smile that sent a thrill through Mark's whole body. He did as he was told. Tofi bound his wrists expertly with a multiple figure-of-eight knot that wasn't tight or uncomfortable but was more than secure. Next he arranged the pillows into one pile and told Mark to lie down so that his head rested on them. The low headboard behind him was surmounted by a convenient rail. Tofi had left a length of the cord running from Mark's wrists and he looped this around the rail and tied it tightly so that his arms were held securely above his head. Tofi was still wearing his briefs, his erection bulged monstrously inside them and

Mark felt it press hot against his stomach as his captor straddled him.

The first thing Tofi did was to reach over and check the security of the knots. "I want to be sure you can't escape" he said, grinning.

"I'd never try to escape from you" Mark promised, limply.

"You don't know what I'm going to do to you."

"What are you going to do?" A faint note of alarm now in his voice. Tofi let the question hang in the air for a while and sat grinning down at his prisoner. Then he leaned in very close and whispered slowly in his ear... "Anything I like."

Trailing his hands along Mark's arms and down the sides of his body he discovered an area, to the sides of his chest and just below his armpits, where he was acutely ticklish and sensitive and he let his fingers linger here, drawing little feathery circles. Mark wriggled and laughed out loud but Tofi kept it up mercilessly. "You are my prisoner now I think. All prisoners must be tortured." With that he began to run his fingertips around and around the pads of Mark's nipples and soon each tender little tit was standing up, proud and vulnerable. Immediately he went to work on them, pinching, stretching, twisting, flicking, all the time chuckling to himself and dropping little remarks... "You love it when I do this ... yes you do, you love it." Mark felt a desperate need to protect himself, but his hands were securely fixed well out of the way and his body was pinned between Tofi's powerful thighs. There was absolutely nothing he could do, but while Tofi's attentions were sometimes playful and sometimes hard to endure, he was quite the happiest prisoner that ever there was.

At length Tofi left his nipples alone and reaching into the bag, brought out a wide sash made of a dark and heavy cloth.

"So now we are going to play a little game" he announced. "You want to know what is in the bag don't you? Well, now you are going to find out, but we do it my way." He tied the sash around Mark's head. The cloth lay heavily across his eyes so that he could see nothing at all.

"Don't be frightened Mark" said Tofi... "it's okay. This is going to be fun, you'll see, I promise it's okay."

He climbed off the bed and Mark heard him shuffling about in the room. He thought he heard the fridge being opened, but wasn't sure. Then Tofi's voice came from somewhere in the room... "Mark, stretch out more, make your legs wider." He was constantly amazed that his situation could become even more exciting than it already was but Tofi was such a master at this and he had obviously done it before. Mark felt the Samoan's eyes exploring his body as keenly as if he were actually touching him and - astonished that it was even possible - he felt even more naked than before. As he followed Tofi's instructions he realised that he was about to come and called out to his tormentor in a pitiful voice. Instantly Tofi was on the bed and his hand was on Mark's cock, squeezing hard with his thumb just below the head. Mark couldn't imagine where he had learned all these tricks, but it was very effective, quickly choking back his ejaculation.

He relaxed again, but his cock remained quiveringly alert. "I know you're a juicy boy" said Tofi, "but you don't dare to make a mess until I say." Mark managed a weak "Yes Tofi" in reply. The next thing he knew something hard and fibrously rough was being rubbed slowly up and down the length of his erection, hurting slightly each time it brushed the exposed head.

"Tell me what this is" Tofi demanded. "If you are right I give you a reward, if you are wrong I give you a punishment." His ingenuity seemed endless.

"It's a coconut" said Mark with confident assertion.

"Clever boy" replied Tofi, and he leaned forward and kissed him luxuriously on his mouth. "There" he said, "that is your reward." The next one was even easier. An ice cube, rapidly melting, was being rubbed all over the head of his cock and down around his balls. 'A-ha' he thought... 'so he has been in the fridge.' He loved it, though the thing was melting so fast he knew it wouldn't last very long. But just to prolong the pleasure he held back from giving an answer until the last cold drops had run away round his groin. His correct answer was then rewarded with another lingering, sensuous kiss.

Then something with a flat, smooth surface was being dragged back and forth across his swollen plum. The sensation was uncomfortable, if not actually painful and he didn't have a clue what it was.

"Come on boy, you must make a guess."

"Tofi I've no idea ... is it some sort of fruit?"

"That is not good enough" said Tofi with mock seriousness. "Now I must punish you." Mark stiffened in anticipation of whatever was coming, but when after a few seconds nothing happened he started to relax again. The instant he did so a spike of pain shot through him as Tofi grabbed his testicles and gave them a squeeze, sharp and quick. He squealed aloud and Tofi laughed.

"Open your mouth" he ordered. As Mark obeyed something soft and aromatic was placed in it and he realised at once that the offending item was a banana. But before he had even swallowed the fruit something with a softer texture was being wrapped around his cockhead, squeezed and rubbed in hard. Parts of it trailed down the shaft and around his balls.

"That's the skin" he shouted triumphantly and they both burst out laughing as Tofi continued to grind the banana skin into his cock. After a while he tossed it aside and Mark heard a curious rustling sound.

"Okay clever boy" said Tofi, "tell me what this is." To his surprise something touched his left foot and began moving slowly up his leg. It felt like some sort of long brush made from wiry hairs but with harder, rougher strips intermingled. It tickled exquisitely as it trailed along his leg, but as it passed over his genitals some of the rough bits snagged on his cockhead causing him little darts of pain and making him flinch. It then trailed off down his right leg, then back again, over and over. The tickling sensation was wonderful and the little snags that came each time Tofi raked it over his cock just added spice. Sometimes Tofi would keep it there and swish it around playfully for as long as he thought Mark could stand it. At length he demanded an answer, thinking he was keeping quiet because he was enjoying it so much, but Mark's reply was a limp confession that he didn't have the first idea. Tofi enlightened him - it was pandanus leaves, dried and torn into fine strips then tied into a bunch. His mother used it to sweep her farlay, but he considered he had found a much better use for it and Mark was not about to disagree.

"Now for your punishment" said Tofi. Mark braced himself for the expected assault on his balls but instead Tofi flicked his cockhead very hard with his finger. It smarted and he yelped from the shock, but Tofi laughed and kept on doing it, over and over again.

Finally he announced it was time for the last object. He reached into the bag and drew out a large pineapple and a knife with a long, thin blade. This he used deftly to cut a cylindrical hole up the middle of the fruit which he then promptly slid right over Mark's erection. Pinching with his free hand at the base of the cock to prevent his foreskin riding up, he began to slide the pineapple up and down in long, easy strokes. For his part Mark had quickly realised what this was. His cock was encased in a sheath of firm, slippery flesh which felt fantastic as it slid over him, but it also contained little rough bits that caused flickers of pain as they passed up and down. Tofi had done it again - he had managed to find that indescribable place where intense pleasure mingled with just bearable pain. Mark was writhing around in rapturous convulsions and both of them were laughing.

"Tell me what it is" ordered Tofi.

"Never" shouted Mark.

"Tell me now."

"Never" Mark laughed and screamed, "I'll never tell you." Tofi stopped his pumping and tossed the pineapple to the floor. "That is no good" he said, "you enjoy that too much." Mark begged him to put it back but he ignored his pleas and instead pulled the blindfold off then rolled over onto his side and removed his own briefs. These he rubbed in Mark's face and he left them there while he untied his wrists. Then the briefs were tossed away and for a while the two men were locked in the deepest and most searching of kisses. Then Tofi sat back and produced one last surprise from his bag.

"This is coconut oil" he said, "very good for the skin." With that he unscrewed the lid, slopped a big puddle of oil onto Mark's stomach and set about spreading it over his body. To begin with he was quite rough, but he soon settled into an easy rhythm of long, slow sweeps.

"Your turn" he said suddenly, handing the pot to Mark and tumbling over onto the bed. Though an entirely different kind of pleasure, Mark enjoyed this as much as anything that had happened that evening. Tofi sprawled and stretched before him, naked, his dark coppery skin smothered in oil. Mark's hands and eyes explored him with extreme thoroughness and a reverential appreciation.

Before long they were wrestling and tumbling around in a slithering, slippery frenzy. Their oily fingers found their way into the crevices of each other's arse cheeks and when Tofi began to stroke and probe his sphincter, Mark thought he would explode with the pleasure of it and he in turn explored Tofi's fundament with equal curiosity and determination. With their fingers sliding deep inside each other, their tongues entwined and their cocks pressed between their stomachs and rubbing together they settled into some kind of rhythm and it was not very long before they both came - at the same moment and with shuddering force. Jism oozed hot between them and mingled with the oil as they continued to slide back and forth.

When at last they were spent they lay exhausted, panting, coiled tightly around each other and they stayed like that for a long, long time. For Mark it was as though their two bodies had merged into one - an indivisible bonded unity of male flesh and spirit.

When at last they tried to move they found that in places their stomachs were stuck together and they had to disentangle some of the fine hairs with great care. But they enjoyed this as it proved to be a gently intimate activity. Soon they were in the shower together, squirting big splodges of shampoo and shower gel all over each other. Pressed together in that confined space the slurping and sliding was irresistibly delicious and it wasn't long before they were in just as much of a frenzy as they had been earlier. This time they did not come at precisely the same moment, but while their ejaculations were smaller they were able to watch each other in their moments of extremis.

They took it in turns to clean each other - by hand, very slowly and extremely thoroughly. Mark spread shower gel lavishly over Tofi's body, scrutinizing every curve and contour, examining the colour and texture of his skin and the springy resistance of the muscles beneath. He was still utterly in awe of Tofi and moved beyond words by the sense of physical kinship that flowed between them with the simplest of touches. As his soapy fingers plied their way around the Samoan's body and his eyes roamed over that endlessly interesting terrain he was lost in the beauty and intensity of it all and in his continuing and overwhelming sense of privilege. When it was Tofi's turn Mark sagged against the wall and gave himself up blissfully and completely as the Samoan, his hands working slowly and deliberately, took possession of him.

When at last they were done they rinsed each other but didn't bother to towel off. Instead they went and sat, side by side, on the balcony. The air was cooler now; not much, but noticeable, and they sat listening to the ocean, each with his hand resting over the other's groin, idly fondling. But they had not sat like that for long when the sky became light and the air full of mist. They were both amazed for it meant they had been playing all night - at least eight hours, possibly more. Mark could not believe he had been so wrapped up in it all that the whole night had passed. He took Tofi by the hand and led him back into the room. They lay on the bed and pulled the sheet over, entwined themselves into a complex and comfortable knot and fell asleep.

Eleven

Mark woke to find himself alone in the bed but as he stirred Tofi's voice penetrated his fog: "Hey sleepy boy, want some breakfast?" He opened his eyes to see his friend sitting cross-legged at the foot of the bed. He was naked and was peeling and slicing the pineapple over some newspaper. When Mark sat up Tofi leaned over and placed a big chunk in his mouth. His teeth sank satisfyingly in and the sweetness was ever a surprise. He flashed briefly on the beach at Lalomanu with Sam, but then a far more urgent image tumbled into his head as he remembered what they had done with the pineapple last night. His cock stirred immediately. Tofi laughed and placed another piece in his mouth, this time allowing Mark to lick the juice from his fingers. They sat closer and fed each other pieces of the dripping fruit, their fingers lingering in each other's mouths and the juice running down their chins. Both their cocks were now lively and when they had finished the pineapple their kissing was deep and sensuous and their sticky fingers found plenty to do.

It was Tofi who stopped it. "Not here" he said. Mark was puzzled. "I've got an idea."

"What are you talking about?"

"You got spare shorts - you know - for swimming?"

"Yes" said Mark, "I've got three pair."

"Then let's go swimming."

Tofi was up and rinsing himself in the bathroom before Mark could respond. "Come on" he said, "it's Sunday, I don't go to work, come on let's go swimming."

"What is your work Tofi?" Mark was taking a piss while Tofi pulled on a pair of his swimming shorts.

"I go fishing for the hotel, for the kitchen. You saw me do

that - you watched me long time." Mark's cheeks flushed and he smiled self-consciously. They both laughed. "And I help my father with the bananas - at the plantation. We load the truck and it goes to Apia, to the market. Sometimes I go too."

"You see, we don't know anything about each other."

Tofi laughed - "I think we know plenty about each other."

"You know what I mean - I mean..."

Tofi cut him off. "That is okay ... I think that is the best thing."

Mark felt slightly foolish. He knew Tofi was right, of course he was right. This was not some schoolboy holiday romance - Tofi was part of the physical world of Samoa, part of the heat and the rain and the loveliness and he sensed that it would be a mistake to think of him too much as a person. Knowledge of Tofi would make him less perfect, more complicated, harder to leave. And he knew that he would leave, but at the moment he couldn't allow that thought anywhere near him.

They were making their way down the short path to the beach. The whole place appeared quite deserted. "But I mean, these games we play ... all this stuff we do together Tofi - where ... I mean ... how did you learn about it all?"

"Well you see, Ili - he is my best friend, since we were babies. We always play together, secret games ... you know ... in the forest. We have always done that. We try all sorts of things, anything we can think of. It's just for fun you know, one day we both have to get married." Mark was taken aback and Tofi noticed him stiffen. "No no, it's okay" he said. "Nice Samoan girl, have children, it's okay, everyone in Samoa gets married, it's what we do. But Ili and me, I think we always play our games, just for fun you know?"

"You mean like a hobby?"

"Yes, yes, a hobby." Tofi laughed. "That is it, a hobby, yes."

Mark already regretted starting this conversation. He saw his games with Tofi as the small tip of a very large iceberg and could only wonder at what pleasures he and Ili had had in their years together. He also had an image in his mind of being taken deep into the rainforest by the two of them to frolic naked under a cool waterfall or be tied to some exotic tree and used all day for their entertainment.

But Tofi was running ahead across the beach, beckoning to him to hurry and catch up and he ran to his friend as though pulled by an invisible cord. They tumbled into the warm water and immediately started wrestling, stirring up a huge commotion as they rolled and thrashed about. Although there wasn't a soul to be seen on the beach they both felt an urgent need for greater privacy; even there in the shallows they couldn't keep their hands out of each other's shorts. "Come on" said Tofi, swimming off. "I know a place, I'll show you."

They swam off towards the rocky point that marked the near end of the beach and once around it found themselves out of view of the hotel. Beyond the point the rainforest came right down to the water, with only the thinnest of sandy strips at the edge of the lagoon. The land there was steep and trackless, there was no-one to see them.

Tofi continued swimming out towards the reef. Mark wondered where on earth they could be going, but followed him like a contented puppy. After a long swim that had started to become quite arduous Mark looked ahead and saw his friend standing up, the water only just covering his knees. Tofi had led him to a coral tower like those he had seen while snorkelling the other day. They were a long way from the shore, perhaps five hundred metres, and the reef was only fifty or so metres in front of them. Following Tofi's directions he swam around the rocks and tried to climb out where his friend was standing but Tofi warned him off. "Be careful" he said. "This coral is sharp, you can hurt yourself. Your feet are not tough like mine, don't try to climb. Take your shorts off and pass them to me." Mark did as he was told. Tofi took the shorts and held them over the coral. "Here, climb up and sit here" he instructed. Mark followed his directions and sat down on the cotton shorts which protected his cheeks nicely from the grazing coral. Tofi in turn removed his shorts, placed them over the coral and sat down beside him. They sat very close with their arms around each other. The water came about half way up to their chests and lapped gently around them.

Tofi took Mark's cock in his hand. Mark found that he could not move very much without scratching himself on the coral so he nuzzled in for security and tried his best to keep still as Tofi, working firmly but easily, made him come. The white strands and blobs floated away in the clear water and they sat cuddling, watching them go. When Mark had recovered his composure he wrapped his hand around Tofi's beefy and splendid sex and treated his friend to the same desperate little intimacy.

As Tofi's jism bobbed away in it's turn into the lagoon they began to notice little fishes emerging from crevices in the rock and sniffing around their toes. They were bright yellow, about three inches long and swam with nervous caution, darting away to safety at the first hint of movement. One particularly brave character approached Mark's cock. They both tried to keep very still as it inched nearer, then all of a sudden it lunged forward and gave him a little peck, right on the head, before flashing off to a safe distance. Tofi burst out laughing. Mark was more indignant as it had actually been quite painful. The little fish came back and hovered again, close to Mark's cockhead. "Keep still" ordered Tofi, anticipating Mark's strong desire to shoo it away.

"But it really hurts" Mark protested.

"Do as your told" said Tofi, grinning and watching the little fish intently. The fish struck again, then vanished. Mark flinched, Tofi laughed and kissed him on the cheek. Then, to his surprise, Tofi reached down and took hold of his cock, pulled the foreskin all the way back and waved it in the water, laughing and calling to the fish to come and have a bite.

"TOFI !!!" Mark yelled at his friend.

"Shsh ... sh" said Tofi, "I want to see what happens."

"But it really hurts!!"

Tofi ignored him and maintained his grip as two yellow fishes came and sniffed around the head of his cock. But neither of them nibbled and when, after some minutes, they swam away Mark's relief was tinged with a certain disappointment. Tofi pressed his face in close and whispered in his ear... "Tonight, I will eat it." He let the words hang in the air as he brushed his nose against Mark's ear. "Then I will fuck you." Mark let out a weak gasp and very nearly ejaculated for a second time.

As they sat quietly together, the warm water lapping gently around them, Mark found himself increasingly compelled by the movement of breakers over the reef. The barrier itself was only visible in the water by the busy froth that hissed and rushed across it. From the shore you could just hear it faintly, but out here it was much more immediate. The reef was many metres wide, perhaps a hundred or more in places. When the swells of the ocean surged against it they bubbled over the top and their force was spent long before they could interfere with the tranquillity of the lagoon.

"You watch it like me" said Tofi.

"Mmm...?" Mark had been drifting away and his friend's voice brought him back.

"The reef" said Tofi, "you like to watch it, to listen to the sound. Sometimes I swim out here and just stare at it and listen to the sound. It is the edge of the world - the edge of our world. Outside is just space. The ocean pushes against the reef but it cannot reach us. Outside is only space ... and movement - always movement - the ocean never stops moving. But here it is still - here we are all asleep I think."

"I think you are more awake than most of the people in my country Tofi."

"When do you leave?"

Mark felt a little shiver go through him, but it passed by.

He wished Tofi hadn't mentioned it, but he knew the pain would come later - after. He knew that he would leave Tofi and depart from this place in a numb and orderly way, only later allowing the loss to be felt.

"Tomorrow."

Tofi didn't answer, he just looked at Mark and smiled comfortingly. "Race you back" he said suddenly and leapt into the water. Startled, Mark followed him and they both had to turn quickly and retrieve their shorts before they floated off. Tofi streaked away and Mark couldn't hope to keep up with him. When he finally arrived, exhausted, the beach was still deserted and Tofi sat at the water's edge, legs apart, shouting encouragement and laughing. Mark swam right up to him, crawled a pace or two and collapsed with his arms around his waist and his face buried deep in his lap. Tofi cradled his head and rubbed his tired shoulders.

"Come on" he said, "better go and have a shower, I have to go soon."

"But it's Sunday" Mark protested, "you said you didn't have to go to work today."

"No, but I have to go to church, then have big lunch with my family. It is our way. If I miss it I am in big trouble - big trouble.

In the shower they again surrendered to each other's hands - each giving his body up willingly to the other's searching fingers as the soap flowed and the salt of the sea was washed away. They kissed and Tofi was gone. The day passed for Mark in a blur of blue. He went snorkelling again for a long, long time. He wandered the beach and when the sun was too fierce he lay on his bed, rolled himself in the coconut oiled sheet that smelled so strongly of Tofi and contentedly dozed the afternoon away.

That night he ejaculated three times in response to the voluptuous but testing ministrations of his friend's mouth. Tofi devoured his genitals expertly and relentlessly for more than two hours and when he finally stopped it was only to turn his attention elsewhere. His strong fingers, slippery with coconut oil, probed and stretched Mark's fundament. Playful, but at the same time insistent and purposeful, they teased away any last shreds of inhibition that lingered within him. It seemed then to Mark that everything they had done together up to that point had been but a preparation. All his silly, terrified, self-conscious, self-absorbed, paranoid stupidness had been torn away and at long last his soul could see daylight. His body cleaved, after rolling on a condom Tofi entered, their flesh became one, and for who knows how long Mark's conscious mind was lost, floating away into a wholly new dimension.

Afterwards they lay coiled around each other, exhausted and breathing deeply. Tofi soon fell asleep but Mark lay there, determined to drink in every last drop of this experience, happily cocooned in another man's flesh and still amazed, despite all they had done together, by the sheer visceral shock of it all.

At last he did sleep, and when he woke it was daylight again and Tofi had gone. A clutch of yellow frangipani blossoms lay on the pillow beside his head; he breathed the scent in deeply and smiled. He was grateful that Tofi had slipped away while he slept. Saying goodbye face to face in the light of day would have been uncomfortable and unsatisfactory. This was so much better - no discomfort, no brave faces, no expressions of sadness or painful hugging. Tofi had just slipped quietly back into the rainforest, or the lagoon, or wherever it was he came from. But Mark was not unhappy - not in any way. He had always known that this encounter would be brief and he understood perfectly now that this was not the end of anything. That on the contrary it was very much the beginning - the beginning indeed of his life - his real life.

Arriving back in Apia he found that Aggie's Hotel was full so he made his way along to the other end of town and took a room at the Tusitala. This was not nearly as homely as Aggie's, but it boasted the same impressive, high vaulted ceilings as the Rainmaker in Pago Pago. Tusitala - Teller of Tales - this was the name the Samoan's had given to Stevenson and it now reminded Mark that he had yet to pay his respects to the great man, let alone to commune with his spirit. Over the last few days he had thought of little except Tofi; he had been more than occupied with everything that had happened and any thoughts of Stevenson, or of the Bounty, or indeed of his book had all been comprehensively swept aside. But as he sat having dinner in the cavernous 'Stevenson Lounge', gazing up at an immense portrait of the man himself, he knew that he must do something about it.

The next day was his last in Samoa. He took a taxi a couple of miles out of town to 'Ala o le Alofa' or the 'Track of the Loving Hearts.' This was a path, cut by local people, that wound it's way through a steaming forest and climbed steeply fifteen hundred feet to the top of Mount Vaea, a good hour's sweaty walking. Here Stevenson was buried in splendid isolation, with a commanding view over the island he so loved.

The tomb stood in a clearing at the summit - two simple limestone slabs, the smaller sitting atop the larger. Mark stood for a while, trying to picture the actual bones lying somewhere underneath. On one side of the upper slab a plaque bore an inscription. It was a poem, one he had known since childhood, though he hadn't known until now that it was written by Stevenson - his own epitaph:

> Under the wide and starry sky
> Dig the grave and let me lie.
> Glad did I live and Gladly die
> And I laid me down with a will.
> This is the verse you grave for me:
> 'Here he lies where he longed to be,

Home is the sailor, home from the sea
And the hunter home from the hill.'

Perfect, he thought - simple and satisfying, poignant but lilting as a cradle song. But could that be right - all that stuff about longing for death? *'Here he lies where he longed to be ... Gladly die ... laid me down with a will...'* It couldn't be true. The man was so creative, a genius - a brilliant, prolific, sensitive, vision-ary genius. He wrote Treasure Island at the rate of a chapter a day! He was positively bursting with creativity and yet his affliction was so terrible that he craved the relief that only death could bring. Mark saw it all now. In three nights Tofi had blown away all the years of accumulated fog; the clarity was as sharp and brilliant as the Samoan sunlight and in it's glare he understood perfectly how profound was the change in him.

Phyllis was right, she was absolutely right - it wasn't the same thing at all. Her words had shocked him, though he had to admit now that he had if only half-consciously - seen a par-allel. But how ridiculous, how moronic to take his silly fear of people and his use of his sexuality as an excuse and compare it - or even to think of comparing it with Stevenson's situation. How could he have seen his sexuality as an affliction - as a curse that stopped him from living? How could he have gone all those years without allowing himself to do what he and Tofi had done over the last few nights? He cringed at the thought and knelt down beside the tomb in smarting supplication.

But his old self was his old self and he was content at the moment to leave him be. His new self was far too excited real-ly to be bothered with any of that right now and he knew that over time he would gradually unravel what had happened to him. He also knew, or at least guessed - hoped - that through that unravelling he would come to find the solutions for William and Jimmy and Thomas and that his book would then start to develop some backbone - some point. So for now he was content just to sit with the writer's bones, survey the coast spread out below and gaze out in to the great Pacific void.

That evening he sat sweltering in the Stevenson Lounge while the rain hung a frothy curtain six feet from his elbow and slapped at the huge leaves of a nearby banana tree. He watched as a puddle filled with two inches of water in less than half an hour. Earlier he had telephoned Mafalu to say farewell and thank him for his hospitality. Mafalu apologised profusely for not having managed to see him again and added rather lamely that one day he would make it to England and would look him up. His flight was due to leave at the convenient time of four in the morning. By midnight the rain had stopped and he ordered a taxi at the desk. Both the ground and the air were supremely wet and the night, once he was away from the town, supremely dark. Apart from a few itinerant pigs and crabs - both about the same size - that were picked up in the headlights he saw nothing and no-one during the twenty squelchy miles to Faleolo Airport. The journey took about an hour - fast by local standards - and he arrived to find the airport dark, deserted and silent. Out on the tarmac a small jet stood with it's engines sealed up. It felt as though the last plane had left here forty years ago and he padded around the eerie spaces like the night watchman in a museum. In one area he came across a group of large Samoans laid out on benches like so many beached walruses, all snoring away peacefully, but apart from them he saw no-one for several hours.

Then, quite suddenly, there came a surge of activity. Lights came on, shops opened, check-in desks opened and people appeared all over the place as though emerging from secret burrows. A minibus arrived with a small party of tourists; the fruit bat was among them, still wearing his mackintosh. Then came a roar from somewhere out in the darkness. The plane had landed in a surge of reverse thrust, en route from Auckland. It was as if the aircraft were surrounded by it's own force field that had sparked the little airport into life as it came within range and as they climbed away into the night, immediately seized again by absolute darkness, he pictured the place switching off, deprived of the plane's energy, and resuming it's natural slumber.

In the next seat was a very large Samoan. So large in fact that his body spilled over the armrest and occupied about half of Mark's space, forcing him to lean to one side and squash himself against the window. The plane was obviously full and there didn't seem to be anything he could do about this so he resigned himself to the prospect of an uncomfortable few hours and tried vainly to go off to sleep. It struck him then that this aircraft - an old DC8 - was identical in every respect to the one which had carried him so thrillingly from Sydney two weeks earlier. Indeed that it could easily have been the very same one. Moreover, he was sitting in more or less the same seat, give or take a row. He knew it wasn't true - the idea was completely ridiculous, laughable - but it was there, ticking away disturbingly in his mind - the thought, the awful, unthinkable thought that maybe, just maybe he had fallen asleep on that flight and dreamed the whole thing. A real life Alice in Wonderland. That he had never been in Samoa, that he had never met Tofi, that the whole thing had been nothing more than a wonderful, fantastical dream. He knew it was ridiculous, completely and utterly ridiculous, but in an effort to reassure himself that he wasn't losing his mind he actually reached into his bag and examined his flight tickets. They of course told him what he already knew - that he wasn't crazy, that he had been in Samoa, had swum in that fabulous lagoon, had spent those nights with Tofi. Tomorrow Tofi would do his work at the plantation then run off into the rainforest with Ili and tell him all about the Englishman he had deflowered, the Englishman whose life he had transformed. It was indeed a dreamworld, but a real dreamworld and he had entered it as one person and - of this at least he really was sure - emerged as quite another.

Several hours later both the night and the flight were

beginning to seem interminable. Mark sat with his face pressed against the window, his mind emptying but yet unable to sleep, unlike the fat man who snored away contentedly beside him. But then a crack appeared in the darkness - somewhere ahead of them a sliver of light, faint but discernible - and it spread quickly out into a thin band of peachy pink. The aircraft was still locked frustratingly in darkness for some minutes yet, but dawn is an abrupt process in tropical latitudes; blazing sunlight poured in as the crack widened and in next to no time they were sailing free in the horizonless blue space that is the oceanic stratosphere and the aroma of fresh coffee was wafting through the cabin.

He had to attempt the buttering of a croissant with his elbows jammed in front of him, but he wasn't really bothered because something much more interesting was happening. In the far distance, somewhere in the milky haze between sea and sky he had spotted some tiny black specks and he knew instantly what they were - Haleakala and Mauna Kea - volcanic peaks of the Hawaiian Islands poking above the morning mist, impossibly remote and ineffably reassuring. When he first noticed them they were still perhaps two hundred miles away and over the next half hour they grew steadily larger as he kept his eyes fastened to them. He had only been in space for a few hours, not days or weeks or months, but these little flecks of land seemed almost unreal to him - improbable in their isolation. The grey-brown slopes of the volcanoes became startlingly clear in the morning sun and the rising mist that skirted them covered a land that could have been - should have been - full of mystery and wonder. But as the plane sank through the dissolving haze and they flew along the coast of Oahu towards Pearl Harbour and Honolulu Mark looked down and saw modern houses and swimming pools and organised, squarely demarked plots of land. For a while he thought he might be either falling into another dream or waking up from one and he really wasn't sure which. Before long Honolulu itself swam into view. He recognised Diamond Head and Waikiki Beach from many a television show, but he wasn't at all prepared for the sea of concrete that greeted his eyes - the grid pattern of wide streets, the shiny cars, the square buildings, the skyscraping hotels, and near the airport, huge steel oil tanks.

The plane returned him inexorably to earth and he stepped through the door into completely different air. Still hot of course, but fresh and light; all that great wetness was gone, all that steam-heat and muddy indolence. Monstrous jumbo jets roared all around him; he hadn't just returned to earth, he had returned to the twentieth century. The airport building was bewildering - a vast, sprawling mass of concrete and chrome, a city in itself, seemingly of science-fiction proportions and full of people racing maniacally in all directions. Wherever he looked people with serious faces were charging headlong. But why did they all look so miserable? he puzzled, and why in so much of a hurry? He felt detached from them, separate, as though he were watching a film or somehow existing in a different time frame. Even stranger to him was the antiseptic cleanliness. He wandered crystal corridors of chromium and glass. Grimy from travelling, he felt like a virus that had blown in from the swamp to contaminate the surgical environment. Seeking comfort in food and drink he wandered into a café, but it was so startlingly, frighteningly clean that he wouldn't have been at all surprised if open heart surgery had been going on over by the delicatessen. He wasn't prepared for this. It just wasn't fair. He wasn't ready to be catapulted back into the real world like this. He found pineapple gift-wrapped in neat, crystalised cubes, not handed to him in sumptuous, dripping slices fresh from the rainforest. He longed for leaf mould, for muddy streets and ancient dwellings. He longed for the musty smell of the rainforest, he longed for wet, womb-like air. Above all he longed for Tofi. But he knew perfectly well that Tofi would always be with him - that he was part of him now. The person he had become was every bit as much the fruit of Tofi's loins as any child the Samoan might sire in the future. More so perhaps as his had been an immaculate conception - a purely male affair. He was now, and always would be a product of Tofi's heart and flesh. He slumped in a chair and allowed the thought to soak through him.

Entering the departure lounge he found a fat Lockheed Tristar humming quietly beyond the glass, baggage handlers and mechanics busy like ants around it's enormous feet. He walked through the airbridge and took his seat. Before long the great monster rolled away from the terminal and taxied awhile, then swung round abruptly, roared, hurtled, creaked, rose into the air, banked slightly over a glittering sea and set sail for San Francisco.

Twelve

The jumbo-jet that carried him on the long flight from San Francisco back to London was sadly in the hands of the same dreary and romantically impoverished airline that had flown him out to Australia all those weeks before. The aircraft's internal seating arrangements were unusual in that Economy Class extended to the upper cabin and it was here, at the top of a spiral staircase, that Mark found himself amid an assortment of besuited middle-managers, all of whom wore the same self-satisfied expressions on their faces because, being seated upstairs, they could pretend they were in Business Class and therefore much more important people than they actually were.

The plane took off and climbed away in the direction of Canada, heading up towards the Arctic on a Great Circle route over to Europe. It grew dark very quickly and after a night that Mark had begun to think would never end they chugged quietly along through a pearly-grey dawn light, far above the North Atlantic. Breakfast came and went, then the stewardess came amongst them distributing Sunday newspapers and the cabin was filled with the sound of gentle rustling. The man sitting beside him was youngish but wore a tie and looked serious. Mark had noticed early on that he had nice hands, but his legs were far too skinny to be of any interest. There was no conversation between them. Once or twice the man threw him a frosty sideways glance that spoke volumes: "Who do you think you are sitting here in your jeans and your sweatshirt?" it said. "You've no business travelling on a flight like this and you're ruining my fantasy that this cabin is for important people only."

On receiving his newspaper from the stewardess the man rifled through the numerous sections, threw *Weekend Leisure* to the floor with a disdainful and irritated flourish and settled back in his seat to absorb *Sunday Business Plus*. Mark was handed a copy of the same paper and in turn rifled through, extracted *Sunday Business Plus*, held it out as though it were an oily rag and made a great show of casting it to the floor. He opened the Weekend Leisure section with a sigh of contentment, held it up high and sat back to enjoy a cover to cover reading.

A couple of hours later the aircraft was plunging through murky and turbulent clouds. When they finally emerged Mark looked out of the window and saw that they were suspended above a dismal and colourless London. He looked forlornly down at an expanse of organised grey and brown and the awful uniform drabness brought a sense of misery into his already dulled mind.

It was a bad landing. The giant craft, so graceful in the air one minute, swooped at the last and cracked into the concrete, returning it's charges to earth with a bone-jarring judder. A reception committee would definitely have been in order. Here he was, returning from a journey that had taken him all the way around the world and it really called for a fanfare, or at the very least a round of applause. But instead he was processed through a disinterested airport that was too busy, too efficient and too clinical to really take any notice of him. He sat on the tube for an hour-and-a-half, jostled by preoccupied people with vacant faces. Again he felt disconnected, detached and entirely separate from them, as though he and they occupied slightly different realities. The train from Liverpool Street took him through the grey, industrial landscape of East London, past grim tower blocks and rows of miserable little houses.

At Maddingly he took a taxi to his house. "Where you been 'a get 'a sun tan like 'at?" asked the driver, cheerfully.

Mark was taken aback and for a moment couldn't think how to answer. Where should he start?

"Oh, well I've ... been to Australia."

"Oh yeah..." replied the driver, without a hint of surprise. He thought the man should have been really impressed, but he wasn't at all, he just shrugged and said that he had thought about taking the wife there but it was such a fucking long way that they went to Barbados instead.

"Ow longs it take then?"

"Oh, I think if you go direct it's about twenty two hours."

"Cor ... fuck me! Nah, ya wouldn't get me up in one of them fuckers for all that time. Ah'd go mad. Still, ah spose if ya get bored ya can always shag one a them trolley dollies eh?" He winked at Mark who stared blankly back at him and shrank into his seat.

"I suppose so" he said, vaguely.

"'Ere, are you all right mate? Not goin 'a throw up in my cab are ya?"

"No, no I'm fine. Just really tired - you know?"

"Yeah - ah should fink you bloody are 'n all. Nuffin worse 'n fucking jet-lag. Cor, fuck me!"

It was more than a week before he was completely free of jet-lag. Night after night he found himself hopelessly wide awake through the small hours. He tried everything - getting up and going for a walk, drinking camomile tea, even sleeping tablets didn't really help. He lay in bed and imagined himself back in Savai'i, floating languidly in the luscious water of the lagoon. But that didn't help either, all it did was to make him think about Tofi and then he would get so powerfully aroused that there was no question of sleep until he had relieved himself, often more than once.

In the evenings he worked furiously on the book, fleshing out the bones of his story with detailed, meandering, poetic descriptions of the Samoan land and airscapes. He felt terribly frustrated that he would never be able adequately to describe in conversation just what the physical environment of a South Sea island was really like. But in his writing he could take his time, could think about it, could mull over phrases and the whole central section of his story began at last really to come alive as vivid and intense recollections poured out of his head and onto the pages.

At work it felt depressingly as though he had never been away. The all too familiar routines were like weights dragging him down and he was plagued by somnolence from the awful jet-lag. All Philmore said was "nice to see you back" before handing him a great pile of work. There was a good deal of admiration for his sun tan and he faced numerous questions such as 'what's Australia like then?' or 'what was the best place you went to?' Edna, who worked on the switchboard said she was really jealous and wished that she could go to Australia because she loved all the tv soaps. Nobody asked him about Samoa. They all knew vaguely that he had stopped off in some funny place but it seemed to be so far outside most people's world that they just focussed in on the fact that he had been to Australia. The stream of platitudes that necessarily issued from his mouth in response to their questions quickly started to drive him crazy and he thought he would explode if he didn't tell someone what had happened to him - or, more importantly, if he didn't start to live as the person he had now become. The people at work only saw what they expected to see - the old Mark lurking behind the sun tan - and this was far more difficult for him to cope with than all his jet-lag or his abiding sense of dislocation.

His mother, after a month of torturing herself with thoughts of him consorting with the dreaded Phyllis, was desperate to reclaim her son, but he was able to use his jet-lag as a credible excuse to keep her at bay and their contact was limited to a few rather strained conversations over the telephone. By the end of his first week at home he thought he really would go mad if he didn't do something and so, after finishing work on the Friday, he took the train to London.

About a year before, he had managed - or so he thought - to summon up the courage at last to visit a gay pub. He had chosen one carefully from a listings magazine on the basis that it looked as if it might have a reasonably discreet location and he sat on the train up to town full of nervous excitement and firmly resolved that he definitely would go through with it. The location turned out to be not quite as discreet as he had hoped, though it was in a reasonably quiet street, but as he approached the building his nerves got the better of him and his courage disappeared like a puff of smoke. He walked past, taking care not to even look at the pub in case total strangers passing by in the street might even suspect that he was gay. At the corner he turned and walked back, this time sneaking a hurried look through the windows as he scuttled past. He knew it was hopeless, that he could not bring himself to go into the pub. He was a lost cause. He gave in to himself and fled the scene, hurrying sheepishly back to the safety of Maddingly and the comfort and consolation of a bottle of red wine.

Today however things were rather different. He deliberately targeted the same pub in order to exorcise the shame of his earlier aborted attempt and he marched up the street with his head held high, strode confidently in through the door, went up to the bar and ordered a pint of lager. It was straight away obvious to him that this was not like any pub he had been in before. It was extremely smoky, which dismayed him; there was nowhere to sit, no tables or chairs so everyone just stood around the sides leaving a great threatening space in the middle. There were no women, only men. He didn't really know why this should have been a surprise, but the fact of it struck him immediately. He took his drink and turned to survey the room. The men ranged around the walls were mostly youngish, but a few older blokes were dotted among them. Some stood in small groups, chatting, but most were alone and they all seemed to be working hard to appear self-absorbed while all the time snatching furtive glances at each other. Anyone having the courage to cross the great space in the middle, either to buy a drink or to visit the loo, was unashamedly scrutinised from head to toe by forty pairs of eyes. Mark looked at these men and tried to hold their darting eyes. If Tofi had taught him anything at all it was that he actually was desirable and that certain knowledge gave him all the confidence in the world. He wasn't frightened of these men, he was one of them. He was also quite convinced that he knew as much about sex as all of them together and that after his nights with Tofi he could take any one of them home and give him the time of his life.

But he didn't like the place. It had an atmosphere of cynicism and predation and a subliminal undertow of sadness that was really quite dispiriting. He finished his drink, took a last slow sweep of the room, just to make absolutely sure that there wasn't any serious talent there and, satisfied that there wasn't, made his exit.

He felt triumphant. His mission was accomplished. Although he hadn't actually engaged with anyone he had at last placed himself in a gay environment - albeit rather briefly - and had emerged unscathed. More than that, he had felt confident and on top of the situation. That particular place had been a bit depressing but he knew there were many others - bars and cafes all over London - and he was resolved now to start frequenting them. He was a man on a mission, secure in the certain knowledge that the gay community would be the richer for his presence.

*

He hadn't seen Gary Dromer since he had been back at work. Someone told him that Gary had taken leave suddenly a couple of weeks before and they weren't sure when he was due back. But as Mark pulled into the car park on the following Monday morning and stepped out into the damp, chilly air he saw the familiar rangy figure striding across and waving.

"Hey, hey ... so the traveller returns. Wow, now that's what I call a sun tan! So how was it then? I bet you're thrilled to be back eh?"

"Oh..." Mark waved a hand in front of him as though grasping for the right word. "...delirious." They both laughed. "Well it's nice to see you Gary, how are you doing?"

"Oh, you know ... so come on, tell me all about it. What was it like? What did you get up to?" Mark looked up at the sky and shook his head. Phew... well... Jesus! Where do I start? There's so much to tell."

"Start at the beginning" said Gary eagerly.

"Oh yeah, well if you've got about four hours to spare."

"Okay, what are you doing tonight? Let's go for a drink ... 'cos I'd love to hear about it." Mark was speechless for a moment, but he quickly got a grip.

"Sh ... sure ... yeah ... why not? That'd be great."

"Do you know the Green Man at Cobbingford?"

"That's the one opposite the church...? Yeah, I've never been in but I've driven past it a few times."

"So let's say I meet you there about eight, how's that?"

"Yeah, brilliant. I look forward to it."

"Great, me too. Gotta rush, I'm supposed to be in a meeting in five minutes. See you tonight then." With that he sprinted off across the car park on his springy legs. Mark couldn't quite believe what had just happened. For all that time - a year and a half - he had fantasized relentlessly about Gary, had played scenes over and over in his mind where Gary asked him out for a drink, wanted to spend time with him, to be mates, to be ... And now it had happened - just like that - completely out of the blue and it would take him time to recover from the surprise. He didn't dare give house room to the thought that tickled at the back of his mind as he knew it would ultimately spoil things. He just allowed himself to savour this sudden and immensely pleasing moment and there was a definite lightness in his step as he made his way in to his office.

The Green Man was a very old pub with a thatched roof - so old indeed that it looked more vegetable in origin than anything else, something that had grown out of the medieval soil and then just sat, quietly rotting. A cosy glow oozed from the windows as Mark pulled into the small, gravelly car park. Gary wasn't there yet and he thought about waiting in his car but quickly dismissed the idea and made his way across. Opening the heavy oak front door he entered a world of red velvet, ancient beams, brass tankards and bellows and bed-warmers, of beer and rolling tobacco, of Stubbs and Constable prints in respectfully heavy frames. He ordered a pint from the kindly barman who looked as if he had been there at least as long as the pub itself. A small group of people sat at one end of the bar, otherwise the place was empty. He chose a seat in a snug little alcove by the fire and awaited Gary's arrival.

He didn't have long to wait, after only a few minutes the handsome figure appeared in the doorway, grinned and sprang across. He was wearing 501's, a tee-shirt and a bomber jacket and Mark thought he looked fabulous.

"Alright? ... What can I get you?" asked Mark, standing and reaching for his wallet.

"No, you're alright ... I'll get it."

"No, go on, this is my round. You get the next one."

"Okay, I'll have a pint of IPA thanks."

Mark hadn't ever seen him out of his office clothes. Gary slipped off his jacket and his strong shoulders flexed as he ran both hands over his close-cropped head. 'He's a white version of Tofi' said Mark to himself, 'and he's asked me out for a drink!'

"Now I'm very curious" said Mark, returning with a frothy brown pint, "you've never asked me out for a drink before

Gary ..... is this some new-found obsession with Australia or something?"

"No, not Australia so much ... that other place you went - where was it? Samoa?

"That's right, Western Samoa."

"Western Samoa ... I mean just saying the name ... it sounds so exotic. I can't imagine going to a place like that, going so far away. What's it like? I mean what's it really like? I want to know everything ... everything about it."

"Everything?" A knee-jerk reaction. He hadn't meant to say that at all, let alone to have sounded so guilty.

"Yeah, I thought so" said Gary slowly, fixing him with a triumphantly amused stare. "It was more than just a holiday wasn't it? Something's happened to you, I know it."

"What are you talking about?"

"You look different. There's no point denying it Mark, you're different. You've got a definite twinkle in your eye, I saw it straight away in the car park this morning and I know that look. Come on, who was she?"

"Look, do you want to hear about the place or don't you?"

"Okay okay ... but you'll tell me sooner or later."

Gary hardly spoke for the next hour as Mark painted an intimately detailed picture of the South Pacific dreamworld he had visited. It all seemed so long ago, yet at the same time he was right back there, his head filled with green and blue, feeling the talcum sand between his toes, smelling the ozone and the coconut oil, hearing the palms rustle in the trade-winds. He felt the sun penetrating him again, felt the solid mass of the rain surrounding him. Gary listened intently, transfixed by his descriptions and floating every bit as vividly in the tropical visions he painted.

"That's about it really" said Mark at length. "I mean, I could go on about it all night but I reckon I've given you a fair idea."

"It sounds incredible" said Gary "and you're a lucky bastard, you really are. I don't think I'll ever get to go anywhere like that, most people never do. You're a fucking lucky bastard, that's what you are."

Mark smiled wistfully.

"Anyway, come on ... what about the rest?"

"What do you mean?" Mark felt his pulse pick up slightly. "You're not getting out of it Mark. I wanna know what you really got up to over there." Mark's heart was racing now. He knew that Gary wasn't going to let this go and what could he do? He certainly couldn't bluff his way through it and chickening out completely would just make him look like an uptight wanker - not helpful when the dawn of a good friendship looked to be on the cards. But he desperately wanted to tell someone - he desperately wanted to tell Gary - to tell him everything, to blurt it all out in a great flood - God what a relief that would be! But how on earth would he react? He had no way of knowing, not really, not to be sure. He wasn't great at thinking on his feet at the best of times and the initiative was sliding away from him fast.

"You're blushing" said Gary.

"I am not" he replied, with mock indignation.

"Yes you are, you're blushing. Your little cheeks have gone bright red."

"Oh Gary..."

"What's the problem?"

"Well why are you so interested? I mean, maybe I don't want to tell you about my private life."

"I don't know, I just ... you know ... I just like talking about it. I mean we're both blokes for God's sake, what's there to be shy about?" Mark met his eyes and held them. 'Fuck it' he thought - 'fuck it!' This is ridiculous - what the hell have I got to be ashamed of? And so what if he doesn't like it? A hundred years from now we'll all be dead so what the hell does it matter anyway? Fuck it!'

"Okay Gary, you win ... but I think you might be in for a

bit of a shock."

"Listen, nothing shocks me mate, nothing. Let me guess ... you've been shagging fruit bats." Mark roared. "Pigs? Goats?"

"Stop it!" Mark shouted, clutching himself. They were both laughing and for a moment neither could speak.

"The thing is..." said Mark, when he finally got his breath back "...I did meet someone in Samoa ... a bloke ... a young bloke ... his name was Tofi and he was the most beautiful man I've ever seen."

"Yeah? ... Well come on then, tell me what you got up to." There wasn't even a hint of surprise in his voice. Mark came within a whisker of bursting into tears. But he didn't, he just sat there glowing inside like a huge, brilliant light bulb. The whole world suddenly opened up before him, in a flash he saw what his life could be like from now on and the relief was a great ocean swell that tossed him into the air and swept him away. He was grinning so hard he could hardly speak. Gary leaned across and spoke quietly - conspiratorially:

"Do you want to talk about it here?"

"Well ... now you mention it, it would be a lot more comfortable at home. Do you want to follow me?"

The next twenty minutes passed in a blur as he drove back to Maddingly with Gary's headlights glued to his rear-view mirror. His breathing was short and he kept saying to himself 'Gary knows I'm gay - he doesn't mind a bit - he's coming home with me to talk about sex!' He said it in his head, he said it under his breath. He thought that if he stopped saying it it would stop being real. His groin was twitching but he fought hard to push those thoughts away. He knew that that was going too far - sliding back towards his old fantasy life and he didn't want disappointment to ruin the pleasure wave he was riding on.

At home he instinctively made for the kettle and the coffee pot but Gary complained so a bottle of Chianti was opened and the two settled comfortably at opposite ends of the sofa. "Cheers" they both said, and chinked their glasses together.

"Now then, where were we?" said Gary. Mark took a deep glug of wine.

"I was telling you about my homosexual adventures."

"Ah yes, and I want *every* detail." He slapped the sofa, hard.

Mark didn't quite tell him every detail, but he did tell him about how Tofi had first fondled him, how he had skilfully brought him off with his toe, how he had taught him so thoroughly to give head, and all about the game with the blindfold. Gary listened closely and kept saying "Wow, you lucky bastard!" To Mark's complete surprise he also said that he thought men probably gave the best head and how could a woman do it properly when she didn't know what it felt like? The mention of the pineapple really tickled him and he blurted out that he had something to top that.

"Yeah, come on" said Mark "this isn't fair. I'm sitting here telling you all this stuff ... it's about time I heard what you and your wife get up to ."

"Well I'm sorry to disappoint you, but we don't get up to anything any more."

"What do you mean ... you sleep together don't you?"

"We haven't *slept* together since our last was born. Two-and-a-half years ago that was."

"But you told me ... I remember ... you said Philmore didn't get his balls in like you and me."

"Oh, that's just my bullshit ... down at the football you have to come out with stuff like that all the time. I can't talk to any of the lads down there about it ... they'd just make fun."

"Oh Gary ... I'm really sorry mate."

"Yeah well ... even when we used to do it I never really enjoyed it. It just wasn't ... you know ... it wasn't what I wanted. I used to think it was, but it wasn't. I mean shagging's alright, it feels nice and everything, but she just used to lie there. We never dreamed of doing stuff like you've done. You're such a lucky bastard! And all these feelings you talk about ... kinship ... emotional solidarity ... I can see what you mean, but I can't say we ever had anything like that. I wonder if a bloke and a woman can ever really have that ... not like you describe. Anyway it's over now, she's kicked me out."

"Kicked you out?"

"Yeah ... two weeks ago."

"Oh Gary..."

"No, we were driving each other crazy, always fighting and shouting,. It's a relief in a lot of ways. I mean I'm round there every day with the kids so they don't really notice any difference ... not really. Do you want to know what did it, what the final straw was?"

"Yeah, go on."

"Promise you won't laugh."

"I won't. Cross my heart."

"Promise you bastard."

"I promise, I said I promise. Come on, what happened?"

"It beats you with your pineapple, I'll tell you. Well, most nights I have to ... you know ... take care of myself, and to tell you the truth I got a bit fed up with it, shutting myself in the bathroom night after night. Anyway, I came home from footie training one night after a few beers ... she was asleep in bed ... I went into the kitchen and there was this small oven-ready chicken on the side. She'd forgotten to put it in the fridge I suppose. Anyway, I was a bit pissed and it looked all plump and pink and I just started ... you know..."

"Gary you didn't? With an oven-ready chicken!!?"

"I know ... it doesn't bear thinking about does it? But I was really drunk. Anyway, she only walked in didn't she. There's me kneeling on the floor with my knickers down and this chicken flailing about on my knob and she fucking walked in!" Both men were shrieking helplessly by this time -

Gary could barely speak and Mark was aching from laughing so much. "She kept a totally straight face.....she just looked at me and said 'You're a sad man Gary Dromer. Tomorrow you can pack your bags and I hope that you and your chicken will be very happy together.'" Mark fell off the sofa at this point and Gary had tears rolling down his face. It was several minutes before either of them could speak again.

"So what's the deal?" asked Mark. "Where are you staying?"

"Oh, in this poxy fucking bed-sit in Chelmsford. It's really horrible but it's all I can afford. I've still gotta cough up for the mortgage."

"Well I've got an answer to that" said Mark "why not move in here. I've got a spare room."

"You serious?"

"Of course. You've got to stay here tonight anyway ... I can't let you drive in your state."

"That's true." He belched loudly. "But I mean ... are you serious? I mean ... have you got room?"

"I just said I've got plenty of room ... and you can pay me whatever you can afford ... I mean ... whatever."

"Well that's fucking decent of you old chap."

"Well I'm a fucking decent old chap ... old chap ... and I'll drink to that. Here's to fucking decency" He emptied what was left of the bottle into each of the glasses and they clinked them together and drained them. Gary sat back and looked at Mark. Mark looked back at him. "What?" he asked. Gary didn't answer, but a smirky grin started to spread across his face and the tip of his tongue emerged, pink and glossy, to slowly circle his lips. "What?" Mark was giggling now. Still Gary didn't answer, but his smile was like sunshine pouring out of his face.

"No ... I was just wondering..." he said at last.

"Wondering what for Christ's sake?"

"I was just wondering ... if you've got a pineapple."